JUDAS TIMES SEVEN

JUDAS TIMES SEVEN

BRIAN BEECHER

AuthorHouse™
1663 Liberty Drive
Bloomington, IN 47403
www.authorhouse.com
Phone: 1-800-839-8640

Published by AuthorHouse 03/22/2012

ISBN: 978-1-4685-5825-8 (sc)
ISBN: 978-1-4685-5827-2 (hc)
ISBN: 978-1-4685-5826-5 (e)

Library of Congress Control Number: 2012903708

1

A SINGLE DROP OF rain fell on the windshield as Bruce Baldwin headed off on his first day as a contract employee of HDB Bank Processing. His assignment was to be a data entry operator, a position for which he is well qualified, having had eight years' experience as a data entry and shipping person at a company which relocated out of the area. It didn't matter anymore what Bruce had done in the past. He was eager to get up and out of his house, as he had recently bought a new vehicle and had the attendant car loan to manage.

He had registered for this job through an agency titled Cadence Office Staffing. A woman named Samantha Simmons handled the account that employed Bruce, for that matter there was a steady stream of Cadence workers in Bruce's area. Cadence was known for its slogan: "We'll Help Maintain the Rhythm of Your Office."

The rain was falling in *buckets* by the time he arrived at work, although it was just over a five-minute ride! Bruce wondered how a mere sprinkle could turn into such a storm so fast. It was the Monday after Thanksgiving, and unusually mild at a time of year when the first snow is often on the ground. Today, the rhythm of the rain was not a welcome sound, as he hadn't an umbrella. The heavy rain was not expected until later in the morning. Surprise! The weatherman had called it wrong once again.

Bruce pulled into the parking lot. His eyes cased his car. Just as he had promised himself he would not do, he'd left his umbrella in the house yesterday after cleaning his new car. With no other choice, he made a mad dash toward the door in a futile attempt not to get terribly soaked.

While standing at the glass entry doors, dripping wet and trying to catch his breath, he was met by a woman whose official position he did not know. They walked to the station where he would be working. There he was introduced to the supervisor of the department, a short, bubbly woman named Paula Brooks. She in turn introduced him to Anna, the one who would begin training until her lead, whose name is Janice Gregory, arrives, which is usually a half-hour to an hour after his shift begins at 7:30.

Anna showed him the men's room and where to hang his coat. He attempted to dry off somewhat and when he returned to his desk there was a hot cup of coffee waiting for him. "A nice gesture," he thought.

The facility ran around the clock, and during peak periods shifts overlapped often, sometimes causing seating shortages. "Don't you just know it?!" Bruce thought, figuring he would have to battle for a seat when the overnight shift didn't leave on time. Chastising himself for the negativity before the first half of the first day had even seen its end, he found both Paula and Anna to be pleasant, and the universe seemed to be sending him happy and good-natured vibes. Anna and later Janice would remind him to always get everything in good order by checking carefully and systematically what needs to be done.

It was very windy and much colder by the time Bruce left for the day. It felt as though it may snow. He was once offered a chance to go to Atlanta, where his former employer relocated. But he turned it down as he had his life situated where he was. Yet in a way he had Georgia on his mind, figuring that it would be somewhat warmer there during the cold winter months which now faced him.

He had just celebrated a birthday with a woman he sees on occasion, and got one little kiss as a sendoff. They have known each other for a few years, but with no plans on taking the relationship to a higher level. Her name is Laura, and she has a house a few miles up the road from where his new workplace is. The product of an abusive marriage, she has two grown sons and one grandson. She discovered a small leak in her roof, and before leaving for work she put a bucket by the spot where the leak was detected. But when she arrived home she was shocked to learn that there was a hole in the bucket, and as a result there was a big mess. She called to see about Bruce, and explained to him what had occurred. On impulse she asked him about fixing a hole in the bucket. He suggested that she might just want to buy a new one rather than trying to fix this one. She was currently on a tight budget and didn't really want to do this, but she would have to get the leak fixed.

Laura was taken with Bruce when she first looked into his eyes. They met through a newspaper personals column. Both were gun shy each in their own way, but have maintained the friendship over the years and once in a while have intimate relations. She is now concerned about the mess in her house because she would like to share hospitality in her home throughout the festive season, and for that to take place she would need to organize the guest room, plan meals, and start now to put up decorations. This was a large list of tasks with not much time to see them through. She finds it hard to believe that soon the calendar would turn a new leaf, and another year would be under way.

As a victim of domestic violence, she has no contact at all with her ex-husband, although she keeps up with his activities somewhat through her two sons. Physically it is over, as a trauma survivor who has had little therapy; it still weighs on her mind a lot. She attends a support group for survivors of domestic abuse. Also, she is facing the frightening prospect of speaking in public about domestic-violence experiences in an attempt to help others over the next couple of days. If she would relax she should be able to get through this task without a problem.

This would also be a period when she may want to talk with whoever is important in her life about whatever is on her mind. Since Bruce has no place to go for the holiday she will have him over for a dinner consisting of a small turkey, apple and pumpkin pie.

2

ON THE JOB, BRUCE would continue to remain focused on the tasks at hand. This is especially important as he has a long list of duties waiting for action. This would be enough to leave him breathless. And then there are all the little things he needs to remember about how the different accounts are to be processed. Janice would go around and give each of the data operators a list of instructions, which get updated at times.

Those who are familiar with Bruce know that he is one who feels he needs to vigorously stand up for what he believes in. The last time he did was at another data entry job where the quota expectations were unrealistic. The operators had quotas of so many actions per hour. They were entering information from medical records, and often one had to hunt and pick to find what was needed. He pointed this out at a meeting on a Friday. The following Monday after reporting he was one of several who were let go.

Bruce was never sure as to whether his speaking up was the reason why he was let go. This was because other operators were let go as well. Management gave the lame excuse for "lack of work" as the reason for the mass exodus. But he is one who recalls when there wasn't all of this political correctness which he feels has gotten very out of hand. Those around him often caution him just to not get too defensive and argumentative, and that it would be best to avoid discussing issues that could escalate into heated debate. Part of him sometimes feels he might have made a good lawyer because he likes to argue points. If he feels another person is right and being treated unfairly, he will bring it on, saying "let it be me who takes the fall, because so and so did not do wrong." He once did just this in a social club he was in during his young adult years, vigorously defending a gal whose name was Dinah, when she was accused of causing problems, even though she wasn't one he was romantically interested in. That incident resulted in Bruce being just barely tolerated, and that was very uncomfortable and bewildering for him.

Before resisting suggestions from other people, or saying no to their proposals, Bruce might be better served by pausing to think about why he is being negative. There are times when he will go as far as calling those who try to advise him liars. Some of this could stem from the fact that he was sent off to a boarding school shortly before his 11th birthday. When he turned 16, a time when most mainstream teenage boys were looking forward to driving a car, he was sheltered in there, and didn't begin driving until he was nearly 26 years of age. Little children had a negative impact on his early life, and as a result he never had the desire to be a parent. Little children called him all sorts of names when he was in public school, and not knowing how to deal with this, his parents pulled him out following the fourth-grade Thanksgiving holiday. It wasn't until about nine years ago that he learned he may have the condition commonly now known as Asperger's Syndrome.

This condition may be responsible for some of his occasional bullheadedness. He may decline advice without giving it due consideration, or because he believes others don't know as much as he, or because he is too fixed in his ways. This is a common trait among those with Asperger's, but if Bruce were asked directly about this, he usually would be in denial. He often felt throughout his life as though he had unreasonable limits imposed on him.

3

BECAUSE OF HIS CONDITION, Bruce is often too cautious in some areas of life, yet not careful enough in others. The biggest handicap tends to come in the arena of social interaction. As a result, it will take extra tact and diplomacy to retain harmonious atmospheres. Cooperating with a mate or partner can reduce the likelihood of dissension, but it has been hard for him to connect with the one person who could color his world.

During the course of his data entry assignment he would be stationed in a work space next to a woman named Robin. She is an older woman, close to his age, and they don't get along very well. On one occasion during a break, another worker told him that an ongoing quarrel or disagreement could be resolved if he was willing to compromise. If not, the two of them could end up in a shouting match.

Bruce wanted to be a believer in compromise, and yet it was hard for him to be able to pull it off. Robin was a single woman in a long-distance relationship which she wasn't very sure about. She has been wary ever since her first love jilted her. Regarding her current situation, she swears that while she may eventually live with him, she won't marry him, as he is one who has a wild side which she is not sure she would be able to cope with in its entirety. At the job she was always asking questions, as she was nearly paranoid when it came to her accuracy. Perpetually broke and also in poor health, she was obsessive about trying to be on the job even when sick. One day she did get sent home following a choking episode at lunch. Bruce and others would often wonder how she did it—maintaining a steady job along with her health problems. Poverty and poor health mix about as well as oil and water.

After the mild spell around Bruce's opening day, the weather took a turn for the worse, with frequent periods of snow and icy conditions in the forecast. This is not a period to drive at high speed, engage in risky sporting activities or display rude behavior. He actually observed road rage on a few occasions, where a driver would flip the finger if it was thought that he wasn't moving fast enough. And although it is the holiday party time, he has no plans to do any drinking of consequence. Police will be out in droves, and spots on radio and television are reminding folks that if you have an urge to ignore the rules of the road, take public transportation or let somebody else drive. This is not an option for Bruce, as there is nothing around that would take him to his job and back. He has never had a DUI, and certainly doesn't want to start now.

4

AFTER SPENDING A LONESOME night at home, Bruce felt somewhat restless. Although he was glad to finally have a job, he nonetheless was crying. He felt as sorry for himself as though life had dealt him a bad hand. Wandering off and doing his own thing might be to his liking. However, the accent now must switch to concentration on financial matters, and this is where focus must be applied. Worry over money matters has plagued him for much of the past year since he suffered two broken bones in a fall at home.

All the dreaming of better days must remain just that—dreams. At times he feels as though the experience at two boarding schools, one locally and the second in California, dealt him a raw deal. By the time he finally graduated at age twenty-five, his life was ten years or so behind where it should have been. He took to desperately seeking a girl to love him, and fell flat on his face in the process. At the time, bars where you could also dance were very much in vogue. Bruce made a few of the "hot spots," but most of the women didn't think much of him, and therefore usually ignored him when he asked for a dance. He was very bewildered by this.

On one occasion where he did get to dance with a girl, he was soon approached by a man who introduced himself as Bobby. "Do you know that you're dancing with my girl?" he asked him angrily. He replied that he didn't, but Bobby was not buying it. Knowing that a fight was about to begin, Bruce summoned the security person, whom he wanted to escort him out so Bobby wouldn't follow him and try to find out where he lived. Needless to say, he never returned to that place again, and for the longest time wondered if this girl had betrayed him. For once he had fun doing a tedious stomp on the dance floor, yet something in the back of his mind told him that she must have a boyfriend, because she pulled back whenever he would attempt to take her hand. He was not, however, prepared for such an irate reaction. But once Bobby began his shouting match he knew that there was no way he would be able to stay.

Although past sixty, Bruce feels that he now has a midlife crisis, feeling as though he has not lived as full a life as he should have. When he would meet a woman who he felt was just his style, she never seemed able to reciprocate. When young he had little success making friends with people his age of either gender. In an attempt to try to belong, he joined a social club for single adults. There were some fun times but he felt that the friendships, if they could be called that, were mostly superficial.

He recently met with a financial counselor at his bank to see what if anything he might be suited for as a self-employed person. He was told that with the economy in the shape it is now in most of the self-employed are experiencing a downturn in business and should now devote time to collecting outstanding debts and money due. And as many of their customers are hurting too, countless of those engaged in small business ownership are seeing prosperity slip away.

Today may be suited for this task better than tomorrow. And yet he would tell himself no following the meeting. He just might have a better safety net in his current position. Besides, when in business for yourself you have to watch for accounting errors. It's then best that you don't delegate your responsibilities to anyone and don't leave cash unattended. Many of those wishing and hoping for the supposed freedom of self-employment are greatly disappointed.

Bruce's love life isn't really a factor at this time. Breaking up with a lover occurred a few years back, probably because ego tendencies, mostly on his end, got in the way of amicably resolving issues. However, he still receives a card from her at birthday and Christmas. He is often haunted by reflections of this part of his life. He often regrets the demise of that relationship and berates himself that he let his feeling of restlessness take over. He is firmly convinced he'll never find anyone better.

Never a huge party animal despite having had his share of fun, Bruce these days is more subdued. If he does go out in the evening, he will refrain from participating in high-risk activities.

5

OVERCAST MONDAY MORNING ABOUT two weeks after Bruce started his job—today's diverse range of influences puts a highly charged atmosphere in the air. Emotional needs are more intense and are likely to remain that way for the next few days. Right now he finds the lead person in his department, Janice, to be a bit overbearing and hard to deal with. That would change later, but for now Bruce doesn't care if Janice is around or not.

Before having acquired this job, he went through quite a long period of unemployment due to his layoff and accident at home. His personal finances and resources as well as money and assets he shares with other people are at an all-time low. His cash flow is now less than usual, and money seems to be disappearing from his checking account at an alarming rate, and he doesn't know why. He is determined to take immediate steps to get to the bottom of this and find out what was going on—was there a person involved or some circumstance he was unaware of? After work he made a visit to his bank in person to question the matter. God only knows why or how this happened, and he needed to find out.

After some scrutiny it was discovered that there indeed was an error on the part of the bank, that an extra zero was added to one of his checks during processing. Credit was given, and relieved, he could now consider this one to be behind him.

Bruce tends to be a walking contradiction, as he is outspoken but at the same time has a tendency to bottle up his true feelings. An open, honest discussion would clear the air and release tension. Whether he is currently solo or attached, romance and desire are often on fire in his life. He hopes one day the spinning wheel will land in the right spot. His current friend, Laura, probably wouldn't be the one he could develop a permanent full-time relationship with. A good enough person, but he tends to have some interests, political and other, that she doesn't share. Surprisingly, neither of them has begged the other to "let it be me." They seem to have a good thing, but there are times when he desires more.

Although Bruce often says he wants to be wanted on a more intense level than he currently is with the one friend now in his life, he often ends up pulling himself back away. On this bitter cold evening, with the temperature around twelve above zero, he would bundle up against the cold and head into the city to have a few drinks and eat. Being holiday party season and knowing roadblocks would be out, he would only drive to the point where he could have access to round-the-clock transit, just in case he might end up being out until close to dawn. He did go to a couple of places where he was able to stomp on the dance floor awhile. But he didn't try the pickup game, knowing it has almost never worked for him.

6

BRUCE SEEMED TO HAVE a rap as being a rebel, one who doesn't really follow the crowd. This has sometimes landed him in trouble, and particularly so in work situations. He is unabashedly troubled by the explosion of political correctness in today's world. Feeling there are so many things that don't seem fair, he would try his best to continue to keep in control and remain safety-conscious. At times he feels that nobody but him would get the kind of reactions which he often does, and a "whipping boy" syndrome has often been the result.

Celebrating having landed what now seems to be a good job, he chose to observe this weekend by escaping to a hotel for one night's stay. He is distrustful of some things in hotels. Therefore, if he is not in his usual environment or while traveling, he would drink bottled water. He would lock the door and use the hotel safe if he is traveling with personal valuables, as he once was a victim of this kind of theft.

When he arrived home following his night away he felt as if he should spend time on household chores. He doesn't want to be rushed closer to the holidays, even though he doesn't have any grand plans for the time. He would clean out the refrigerator, remove out-of-date food from the pantry, and make a list of what he needs to buy.

Thoughts would then turn to furthering his career aspirations. He knows that this may require going back to school to learn updated techniques, to finish a degree, or to obtain higher qualifications. But he questions the wisdom of returning to school at his age. Not only the thought of having the burden of a loan he may not be able to pay off in his lifetime, but later in life it tends to be harder to retain information and learn new things. It might even be a bit like learning do-re-mi all over again. This is something he feels should happen only to those who, say, develop serious brain injuries which create substantial memory loss.

7

BRUCE WAS GLAD TO be busy after a few weeks of relative idleness. With holiday celebrations moving ever closer, taking it easy and relaxing may not be an option.

Janice Gregory, meanwhile, the lead person in his department, has her share of pre-holiday tasks to achieve as well. She just assumed her current position in September. Prior to September her job had been primarily a trainer. An average build, African-American woman of thirty-five, she now has three daughters. The first two had one father, the third a different one. She has never been officially married. She had her first love at sixteen, one who treated her rather badly. She had another suitor over the past summer that also was much less than ideal for her. But right at the moment she was in the middle of decorating and making minor home improvements which she began on a stormy weekend back in September. She could offer hospitality in return for assistance from those she knows.

She indeed would invite skilled family members and friends to assist with do-it-yourself tasks. When the work is completed, she would provide a delicious meal as a way to say thank you. She would add a touch of spice to the food and her guests would be bound to rave about her cooking expertise.

There is always extra correspondence over holiday season. And happy communications received from loved ones and friends currently living in other areas can be a special blessing. So many people nowadays are poor correspondents that it seems there is about a million to one chance of hearing from them. But as Janice hasn't heard from such people recently, she would write and get in touch now. She would build up her courage to write the cards out this evening. Tomorrow would herald a return to the work grind.

There was the thought running through her mind that she just might be attracted to Bruce.

8

JANICE WOULD FIND THE new day to be quite demanding. Today appears to be all about work and business matters. She might need to put in longer hours on the job because of an ever increasing workload and also an ever-decreasing bank account. When she finally got a chance to catch the wind nightfall had set in making the ride home worse as she would have bulky rush hour traffic to deal with.

As he was a temporary but not part-time worker, the luxury of selecting the hours and days he wants to work may not be an option for Bruce right now. The facility operates round the clock with three shifts, and while closed Christmas Day, it was announced that they would remain open New Years' Day. This was due to the landing of a major account fairly recently, not too long before Bruce had arrived there. He hopes he not to have to work that day, but knows that as a new worker he probably will.

His immediate boss, Janice, and other higher-ups at work all seem to have gotten out of bed on the wrong side this morning and Bruce would get the notion that everything he would say or do might be wrong in their eyes. He would have the last laugh later on, but for now he found Janice to be very hard to deal with. He thought it best to carry on with all of his own duties and do his best to ignore her bad humor. Knowing very well that in today's business climate only the strong survive, he would now do his best to bite his lip and focus on the tasks at hand.

Upon his arrival home, Bruce would make a phone call. A trip to the dentist would be in order, especially as he has been suffering from an occasional toothache recently. It would be a couple of weeks before he could get into the office, but an over the counter pain reliever was recommended in the interim. He was really hoping that the pain would just fade away.

9

BRUCE OFTEN FEELS AS if he was born too late. He longs for the type of life not easy to accomplish these days—the life where a man holding even a mundane job like his could earn him enough to take women out on the weekends and not have a big strain on the wallet.

Wishing and hoping the right person will come along can be both comforting and disquieting. Doing what he enjoys assumes importance on most days. He is looking for one who would enjoy a long walk near the water, dancing, and other fun activities. His current friend Laura doesn't seem to enjoy a lot of that even though they have enjoyed intimacy on occasion. She works very early hours at a hospital cafeteria, a schedule not really conducive to activities such as dancing and listening to music, which Bruce really enjoys. His economic situation is forcing him to cut back on so many things, and this has really plagued him.

Laura is not a pretty woman, and shows her age in a lot of ways. Not only was she the victim of an abusive marriage, but she also had a gout attack which took its toll on her physically. But Bruce is really not seeking out great beauty, although he does fantasize about it at times. Words of love are hard for him to express, but they seem to be on Laura's end as well. At times he does wonder how she would react if he chose to pull the plug on their relationship. Neither have the money available to sustain any kind of whirlwind social life. While he has been unemployed much of the time since fall, she recently had a cut in hours at her own workplace.

Bruce is a veteran of the singles dance scene, but lately has had no desire to get back to that arena. The last few times he went he found most of the ladies didn't really want to dance unless the person had that Prince Charming potential, which he obviously lacked.

Working his way back to his former life following the fall has not been easy, the most unfortunate aspect being that the economy hit the skids at about the same time as his recovery. To compensate, he would tend to spend some alone time in meditation. Or he may experience a sense of fulfillment by creating something of beauty, which can provide the pleasure he seeks. Or, he may accomplish this by cleaning the house from top to bottom.

Issues connected with income or values would often cause some upset for him. He would find the need to put things in perspective to keep petty irritations from getting under his skin. He has much disdain for a workplace culture in which so many put on the disguise of friendship while working against you behind the scenes. A part of him would rather be on his own, but is keenly aware that the self-employed person could often experience a delay or postponement of expected cash. He would need to take care not to hold on to ideas that are not supported by facts.

10

A REFLECTIVE PERIOD WOULD set in for Bruce. He would spend some time this week in the mode of rethinking his goals and what makes him happy. Those around him have mentioned his tendency to dwell on certain issues just a little too much. Earlier in his life these tended to be surrounding women and dating. More recently it has been concerning issues that involve the larger society. But when a friend would begin to try to convince him to make a move that he is not comfortable with, he would balk almost immediately, preferring that the soul and inspiration for any moves come from within. He would be honest about his feelings, and not back down. When he follows his intuition and what he feels in his heart, things usually work out for the better. But this has not always been the case. Several years ago he developed a love for his best friend's girl, which created an awkward situation. He now reasons that it happened because he had been lonely too long before that.

While the holiday season is a favorable period for one to spend money on home, family, or a lover, Bruce is in a fairly unique and somewhat fortunate position. For much of his life this actually was the least expensive season for him. When heavy into the dating scene he usually got a break during this time when the women were busy with family activities and largely unavailable for dating. But most of the time he did end up having some place to go at the time of the major holidays.

As Janice was lagging behind with her holiday shopping, this evening she would begin the task in earnest despite having had a hard day on the job. She would then start stockpiling supplies for the big day, all the while taking care to keep things hidden from her three girls. The two older ones in particular have become a very curious pair, to say the least. Not having a large budget forced her to limit gifts to two apiece for each of them.

Following shopping, Janice would be heading out for a night on the town. She is basically a free woman right now, following a long-term relationship with the father of her youngest child. No longer happy together, they split some time back. In her younger days she had a trait of partying fairly hard. But she is no longer such a young woman and has the girls to set an example for. Therefore she should bear in mind that everything is fine in moderation. In midnight confessions, however, she admits to a handful of activities back in her partying days which today she is not proud of.

11

THIS WOULD BE A generally good period for Bruce. When he is on the job, organization and goal setting could be an ongoing theme. He often would snap his fingers in order to get the attention of either Janice or Anna so they could explain a procedure to him. But he is not near as inquisitive as is Robin, the woman in the adjoining cubicle. A morning team meeting, where department goals and expectations were outlined, should prove to be productive. Solutions to problems were likely without too much difficulty or dissent.

Today was the day on which new locker keys were given out. For this Bruce would need to pay a visit to the facility's general office manager, Jennie Mulcahy. She was a bit hurried on this day, as purchasing gifts for business associates and colleagues were on her agenda. She was able to have fun with this task today. She was told to just watch how much she was spending, especially as she had promised to stick to a set budget.

Bruce marveled at how well Jennie was able to fly thought this seasonal exercise. In casual conversation she mentioned to him that you know how it is, the holiday season is now here and then it will be gone. She then handed him his new locker key. All personal effects must be kept in these lockers during the work day except for a pouch in which one could keep small items.

Once he received his key he was ready to head back to his work station. Janice wondered why he was away as long as he was, and he explained to her that he had to wait while Jennie did some other things.

A fascinatingly attractive woman named Michelle walked out onto the floor at that moment and needed to confer with Janice. Well-dressed with neatly manicured nails, Bruce considered her quite attractive to say the least. He thought that if he could get together socially it could be a fabulous encounter for him if she was a solo woman or disastrous if she were an already partnered woman.

12

IT ALSO PROVED TO be a trying day for Robin, Bruce's colleague at the next station. A friendly, yet often intense person, she eagerly looked forward to break time so she could have her cigarette, not being able to break the tobacco habit. She also had some serious health issues, and on this day she would nearly weep as she talked about this. But because she was so broke she had to make like a modern-day Lou Gehrig, always on duty despite her conditions. It may have been a beautiful early winter morning outside, but it was not so as far as Robin was concerned. As the day gets underway she would not have as much energy as usual. Responsibilities and problems would be weighing on her heavily, and everything she tried to do would seem to be taking too much time and effort. Daunted by her attitude this day, Janice would summon her to come to the adjoining room where she would lock the door and she could let it out away from the other workers.

Janice informed Robin that it isn't a great thing to let other people in on her secrets because they may not be able to keep the revealed information to themselves. Conversely, she would need to guard what she says so that she doesn't accidentally send out the wrong message or divulge confidential data. She would close out the conversation by advising Robin to shake off any resentment or jealousy that she may be feeling and focus on all the things that she has to be thankful for.

But Janice has her own set of problems. As a mother of three girls she has a super-responsible role to play. The oldest one will soon be of the age at which she will have to tell her about the birds and the bees, which won't be much fun. And today she also has a new worker, a young Latin lady named Lupe, whom she hopes will be one of her better operators. And she still has the reports she has to turn in to Paula at the end of the shift.

13

BRUCE WAS SHAKING ALL over when he awoke the next morning. He hoped he wasn't coming down with some kind of fever which could cause him to miss work. He recalls the flu bout he had right at Christmas two years earlier which caused him to miss all holiday gatherings. It turned out that the heat at his residence had malfunctioned, so he would huddle tightly under the covers until the heat was restored, and then he was fine.

It was Saturday, and the following Monday there would be a holiday grab bag at work which he needed to purchase for. Gifts could not exceed $20.00 in value. As soon as he had warmed up he headed out to a discount department store where he found an item he thought would be good for the occasion. He then told the clerk to wrap it up, that he would take it. Of course, gifts have to be appropriate for the particular person he was assigned to, and he'd have to hope for the best.

Although grateful he now had a job, tense moments still persisted due to ghosts of jobs past, where some comments he may have made were taken out of context, and he ended up falling victim to the "I got you" trap and ended up being reported. Anger issues continued to arise as they did this morning over the lack of heat in his building.

He knows that if he is still annoyed about something that happened in the past, it is now time to forgive and forget, although that is not always easy for those born under the sign of Scorpio, which he is. If he cannot do anything constructive about something that happened a long time ago, it might be best that he move on. He would be best served by taking the walk, don't run approach—that is, to take time out to meditate and get in touch with his feelings and not spend time brooding. And yet he can't help but wonder if history is deemed to repeat itself and he would be back to square one someday.

Across the street from Bruce there would be a party this evening and he chose to pull himself up by the bootstraps and go. He hoped to act and look his best, even to the point of being able to turn women's heads when he would walk into the room. A sunny mood would return by the afternoon to match the clear early winter sky against the soon to be setting sun. Now mixing with people he could enjoy can be a blessing.

The party would begin at eight, which gave him a few hours to get ready. Despite all the preparation to look his best, socializing would turn out to be stressful this evening as someone there decided that it was fun to annoy him. There was one woman there who tried to be the queen of the party. When Bruce took a liking to her a couple of other guys got jealous and kept taunting him. He didn't know if one of them was her lover or not, but he didn't choose to find out. He went home early.

14

SURPRISINGLY, BRUCE WOULD FIND the following day to be uplifting. He would read the Sunday paper and just putter around the house until twelve-thirty, when he would begin to engage in what promised to be an eventful and busy day. The Sun has now entered his sector of communications, and will bring a more practical tone to the atmosphere. For one, he expects to be working harder now. He will have off on Christmas Day, but nothing extra including New Years' Day.

At the same time Janice is filled with her share of business as well. At this season she doesn't have a special man in her life, and has vowed that she will not ever again be anyone's puppet. She will be the one running errands and finalizing many details for the upcoming festive celebrations. Although doing this will be time consuming and hard work, she would consider it a pleasure and is unlikely to complain, at least not too loudly. Taking the week off from work would help.

Over the next four weeks she plans to work a reduced schedule. This would give her the opportunity to enjoy exploring her own locality, although the area where she lives is admittedly not the greatest. But she may even want to arrange a short weekend retreat or reunion at a site not far from her own base.

Her locale is an urban city neighborhood not far from the real ghetto. With three girls to concern for one might think she'd want to move to a nicer area and would even be a fool for not doing so. But she remains largely because of her family, especially her grandmother who for the most part raised her growing up. Next June she will celebrate a landmark birthday, and Janice hopes to organize a special gathering to celebrate. It would be an uplifting celebration of her life to be sure. But in the present nothing would change the fact that every day brings on new challenges both in work and personal spheres.

15

IT WAS NOW A dynamic time for Bruce, who now felt as if positive energy was in force and as if he in turn will feel positive and energetic. He hopes to be able to make good use of this surge of power to catch up on outstanding tasks requiring urgent action. Personal considerations are in focus, which is how it should be now with a newfound sense of confidence sliding through a carousel of events.

Janice was to be off this week, but came into the office for a time to show her three girls where their mom worked and to deliver some treats to the crew. She declined, however, to participate in the holiday grab bag which took place on this day. However, she would also need the time to devote time and attention to family matters. In the New Year she would consider taking positive steps regarding a new class assignment or an interview for a new job which can advance her position. She heard through the grapevine that a new department was going to be created sometime after the start of the New Year.

For Bruce's part, he was glad he wouldn't have to deal with Janice for this week, as he at this time considered her to be overbearing and couldn't understand why she would switch him from account to account and procedure to procedure as much as she did. As he learned that she had just assumed the lead position in September, he wondered how she knew so fast what accounts should be processed when. Determined not to let himself be taken for a fool, Bruce was determined to rely on his ability to communicate and express himself in an articulate and powerful manner. He felt that doing so would promise good results from interacting with friends and strangers alike. He always tried to display the sunny side, and once he knew the procedures he would on occasion be able to help one do what was needed, even if such was not encouraged. Robin often would ask him how something should be done whenever Janice or Anna were not around or busy.

16

AT THIS POINT BRUCE indeed felt like a fortunate one. Not only did he manage to land a job at a time when many were not able to, at least for now he also felt he was around people at least more friendly and helpful than where he was at previously. He strived to be helpful to others as well as himself. While his true life story was not filled with one success after another, for now he felt as if time was on his side and he was now in a place where he could be successful and grow. He hoped to at least be offered a permanent job after his tenure with Cadence ran its course. He now looked forward to getting up early in the morning to prepare for the new day and work hard on boosting his own self-esteem and confidence. Changing behavioral patterns or applying some restraint may be required if other people consider his actions a display of excessive pride or arrogance. Interestingly, these are some of the traits he heard applied to Janice during her week off.

Many times in an office environment things surface which are meant to be kept hush, and certainly this was the case with some of what Bruce overheard regarding Janice. At the time he agreed for the most part with the sentiment then expressed. So often one thinks that everybody loves them or at least respects them only to find out later that this is not really the case, like a false-hearted lover telling someone you love them but yet despise behind the back.

Shortly before he obtained this job he would receive emotional comfort listening to someone he respected who was offering advice on self-empowerment and the way to obtain greater personal contentment. He had become so used to receiving bad news of one sort or another that he was afraid that he was becoming numb to it. Although not a regular churchgoer he learned about a walk-in ministry in his area. This facility offers no-cost help for many types of personal issues. He went to a local office for some help following his injury, albeit reluctantly.

A sixth sense within him told Bruce to expect the unexpected this morning, and that this may very well involve business associates or the company he now works for. He thus made himself ready for whatever came down. Sure enough there was a brief meeting during which Paula, the department supervisor, confirmed that they would be open on New Year's Day as dictated by one of their new clients. She also encouraged the staff to do their best while Janice is away. The thought of having to come to work on New Year's Day didn't sit well with him, but he did possess the willpower to be prepared to look with fresh eyes at circumstances and arrangements that he had been taking for granted for a long time.

After work Bruce would stop off for a quick meal. There was a moon out on the cold, crisp night by the time he left the restaurant to head for home. He would then put on the TV for a time, take a hot bath and head for bed.

17

JANICE WAS EXPECTANT OF a good holiday period. The father of her two oldest girls, who had been largely absent from their lives recently, paid a surprise visit and brought the girls some gifts. She would focus on priorities. As she has waited too long to get going due to work priorities, last-minute Christmas shopping was on her agenda. She might finish it quicker if she went alone, which is what she did. She would drop the girls off by her aunt. It was now apparent that all were eagerly expecting the arrival of Santa Claus. Before leaving she would write out a list so that she knows exactly what purchases she wants to make. The visit by the father of her two oldest girls, Krystal and Jamicia, was an unexpected development in a less than satisfactory situation. She hopes that this could increase the rapport between the girls and their father. How sweet it is, Janice thought to herself, that James Duane actually brought gifts for them to enjoy.

Social activities should now be enjoyable, heightened by a rush of excitement. Janice now had the feeling that anything could happen, and this could very well be the case. She learned that a distant uncle might pay a visit, and so she would make sure to have the guest room ready in case a friend or an adult relative arrives unannounced as a special Christmas surprise.

And that's exactly what happened. Around nightfall her Uncle Jerome, whom she hadn't seen since she was 24, made his surprise appearance. She was happy to see him, to say the least, and was proud that she had the intuition to have the guest room prepared. And although it was a development she was for the most part unprepared for, she was by no means sorry that he came. They would spend a few hours catching up on all that has happened since she saw him last, talking about each other's personal history.

Bruce now felt as though it was a wonderful world because he now has some steady income again, even though he has no special plans for the holiday other than going by Laura's for dinner around 1:00 p.m. Christmas Day. The jadedness he has often experienced had now subsided, at least for the time being. The only child of now deceased parents, he was glad to be blissfully free of having to deal with the seasonal shopping frenzy. He has always heard about how often single people get depressed at this time of year, but somehow this was never significant in his life.

18

THE BIG CHRISTMAS HOLIDAY has arrived! As Janice was entertaining guests, she could expect a very lively dinner. Many of the folk in her community may feel as if they are deeply connected with their spiritual and religious roots. Janice is not so much so, even though she and the father of her two oldest girls did attend a seasonal concert of carols a couple of nights back. She feels a twinge of regret that she has not participated in this aspect of the season, and those everyday people who surround her have suggested that it would be a wonderful experience to express these feelings and this energy by sharing the day with her own loved ones and extended family members as well as other people who are away from their relatives. She and the three oldest girls did participate in a volunteer food drive to feed the area's hungry. It was a success, and they received enough food for about a thousand dinners. Hopefully nobody will spend this holiday hungry.

Her aunt was actually the hostess for the day's big meal, but Janice did much of the preparing. The aunt particularly enjoyed doting on the youngest child, Serena. Upon her arrival she screamed out "Here comes my baby!" The Christmas tree contained all the usual decorations, and was embellished by a large star at the top, symbolizing the goodwill of the season.

Regardless of how much effort one may have exerted to make the day progress without disruptions, you still need to prepare for such a possibility. However, if handled peaceably, this would just add to the excitement. Some people, once they get their double shots in them, become agitated beyond belief, and just last year there was a Christmas shooting just a block away from her. What is supposed to be a season of joy and goodwill always has the risk of turning violent once the wrong buttons are pushed. She is grateful that no such tension would escalate at her family gathering and that peace was retained.

Bruce, meanwhile, is usually steady as a rock during the season. Laura extended an invitation to come for an early dinner, one of two she would host this day as members of her family were coming by later on. As a worker in a hospital cafeteria she works every other weekend and at least two or three of the year's six major holidays. She was off this time, but like Bruce probably will, she will be working New Year's Day. They had an enjoyable meal, but at some point she would need to make sure she got a chance to put her feet up and relax before her second set of guests arrived. At that point the two of them would spend some time talking before Bruce went home, where he would spend the rest of the day and evening.

19

IT WOULD CONTINUE TO be an exciting time for Janice. If she thought that she could relax and have a restful day, she may need to think again. She would try to make the day ahead as stress-free as possible by clearing away the festive remnants early, then getting some fresh air as the weather was reasonable, with thawing conditions forecast following a clear and cold holiday.

Visiting and chatting with friends and relatives would keep her happily occupied. Although the fathers of her girls had been bad to her in the past, she was grateful that they remembered the girls for the holiday and that she was able to take the week off in order to allow her some time for living. She would find that the week slips by faster than imagined and she'll need to get back to the grind soon enough. Little did she know that come evening she would have a surprise visitor, who would provide an unexpected dynamic she was ill-prepared for.

When the doorbell rang Janice was surprised to see an old friend, Pam, at the door. They were quite a pair back in their heavy partying days. They used to on occasion borrow each other's shoes to match their outfits. And although the Pam and Jan show was quite the thing back in the day, the latter woman would need to defend her views after Pam said something stupid while taking part in a lively discussion around the kitchen table. Even though this would test her communications skills, she did enjoy the experience. That is until Pam accused Janice of not returning one of her pairs of shoes. Up until this point, Pam was trying to lure Janice out for the evening. She had not long ago met a man who just moved to the area from New York City whom she seemed flipped over. But before long the argument over the shoes escalated to a shouting match, with Pam threatening to break through to the closet. By now Janice told her to start walking, saying that she would call the police if she didn't obey.

Following the confrontation Janice would allow some time to regroup, but was so unnerved that she almost broke down, but told herself that big girls don't cry, especially around their own children. Eventually she would settle down to talk, sing, and play board games, remembering to include the younger folk.

20

WHILE BRUCE WANTS HIS life to be purposeful, he is constantly plagued by the apparent specter of fake friendship he has seen around him. Those who will continuously say "how are you, take care etc." yet not really mean it. On this morning his ruler was the concern that in spite of his life being alright for now, that as he enters the industrious sign of his current work environment he will once again fall victim to these trappings. So most of the time his mindset is that he will need to be extra vigilant over the next few weeks in discussions with other people—doubly so within the work environs. He suspects that there is some mean woman there who has enough leverage to be his undoing. But to a large extent this has been true in the social arena as well. He has one lady friend currently and has had others, including one who took some care of him following the fall he had. But the current time frame finds him for the most part in a world without love.

Daunted by certain demons has often led to thoughts of writing his true story for the world to see. A few years back he had a woman who truly loved him. Her name was Lorraine, and they had a relationship lasting over three years. But it was he, not her, who was not willing to totally commit. It was a decision he probably will regret for the rest of his days.

Discretion is not usually his forte, but it may be essential now. Even though what he were to say may be right, he could inadvertently wound others by a sharp tone of voice and hurtful words. This is a pattern that, much to his chagrin, seems to have been repeated often during his lifetime, causing him loads of grief and bewilderment. When going out to socialize he would be baffled as to why a lady he might be interested in wouldn't talk to him. As a result he has, for the most part, avoided that scene, relying more on conceived methods of meeting, such as personal ads.

Bruce would also need to guard against impulsive decision making. Carefully thought-out decisions usually have a better chance of being proved correct. He should be glad all over that he now has a job when many of those around him don't. Yet he feels as if he has to always be on guard for the shoe to drop. But he would strive to allow increased energy and enthusiasm to allow him to work harder to advance his current aims. He looks forward to giving a performance that's right down Broadway.

Yet inside he knows that despite occasional bouts of bravado his lack of resources would leave him too weak to fight if adversity rears its ugly head.

21

SOMEHOW BRUCE WOULD REMAIN energetic. Never having been part of the "in crowd," whether in work or social situations, he had to improvise in order to have substantial life experiences. Energy and enthusiasm are at a high peak at present. He would take the time to ensure that he has not missed out on any real promising opportunities. He often wishes he could fly away somewhere but is really put off by the way airlines are treating their customers these days, so he has chosen to delete that from his radar screen.

Feelings that he has experienced recently may seem stronger, leading him to actively seek someone or something that can provide added meaning to his life. Since Lorraine has been gone he has on occasion felt the void of having someone to love him unconditionally. She is now in another relationship and knows the odds of winning her back are slim to none. It's made all the worse by the realization that *he* was the one who messed up.

Then there was Bonnie, a woman he dated for a few years now about a dozen years in the mirror. When she and her husband married the Elvis song "Can't Help Falling in Love" was their song. That marriage dissolved, but did produce three daughters. When the two of them dated there was never any romance, and he chose to faze this woman out because it was a very expensive affair as she enjoyed upscale restaurants and things Bruce could no longer afford.

But in lacking diplomacy it seems that he always has to watch what he says. There is a strong likelihood of accidentally blurting out something that was supposed to be kept in confidence. In hearing about all the celebrities who have gotten caught in these traps, he assures himself that he wouldn't want to be in the limelight. Although part of a couple of social networking sites, he seldom posts on them, at least partly out of fear of not wanting his whole life exposed and so many words and actions being used against him.

Feeling accident prone would cause him to be alert for all careless action and ready to take evasive measures. And while he would like to be a runaway from many of life's stresses, he is reminded to not speed if he is behind the wheel. On this day off visiting out-of-town friends could appeal—something he has not done since before the fall he suffered through.

22

JANICE WAS UNCERTAIN AS to what would be in store when she returned to work. Although she currently had no significant person to hold her tight during the holiday period, she felt it was a worthwhile time. Today's influences would bring a number of problems that would impact whether she will proceed to sail smoothly through the day or encounter troubled waters. During the week she was not on the job she would find home comforts calling loudly. She would, in addition to the shaking atmosphere of holiday gatherings, take care of domestic chores. She would find that the more she did the more family members were likely to pitch in and help. At one point the girls played a little game with her when they would try and hide from her. She would then urge them to come a little bit closer. They then took a few steps, finally then coming to her. She would remember when as a child she would play hide and seek with both family members and playmates.

An issue that had been simmering in the home and family environment would now boil over. It seems that some of the elder members of her extended family called Janice on the carpet for not attending church more regularly, even accusing her of being a non-believer. She would address the problem quickly to diffuse tension and clear the air. She did so by stating that one of her resolutions could be to attend more, all the while adding that you can express faith in other ways, and that religion isn't everything in life.

She received an invitation to go out, but chose to decline, saying that a night at home enjoying the company of loved ones, reading a new novel, or having a long soak in the tub could be an attractive alternative to going out to mix with people she doesn't know well. And she would work all of these into her evening's agenda. There was a time when going out to party and have fun was top dog. But having three kids and a responsible job has cut into that.

23

JANICE FOUND HER RETURN to work manageable, but with much to do. Her spirit was good but not spectacular. On the home front this would be more a day of preparation than productivity as she busily goes about efforts to organize an end-of-year celebration. Although the holiday season has been extremely successful until today, some domestic friction could now occur. She has learned that her father, now in ill health, will be returning to the area to stay with her aunt. She would remember when, while growing up, he would tend to disappear for days at a time. Her mother was rather neglectful as well, and she was primarily raised by her grandmother. She now didn't dream that the splendor of the season would be disrupted when someone close to her emotionally would be more annoying than usual, and she might not be able to do anything about it. Her aunt is insisting that she help with much of the errand running which will be required.

Janice would be truthful and tell her aunt that she is both a career woman and a single mother. She determined herself to be prepared to explain an offbeat idea or scheme as she knew her aunt could vigorously challenge her viewpoint. After all, how could she be sure that she would not be totally taken advantage of? But once she got a clear head she knew that she had to accept that things are constantly changing, and this was just one example.

She knew she really needed her aunt. As the relationship with her father had been so strained since her childhood and had gone wrong even more lately and something may be in need of repair, this would be a good time to mend, patch, and restore. She missed being held by both him and her mother when she was a child, but now she couldn't wait to hold him and do her best to forgive during what are most likely his final days. For this one-time party girl staying at home with loved ones could again appeal, as she felt physically drained.

24

JANICE WOULD LOOK FORWARD to a much better day than yesterday as the year comes to a close. She is now in a joyful state and a relaxed, happy atmosphere prevails, with energy improving as the day ensued, Janice having so much on her busy mind and too much to dream last night nonetheless.

Meeting someone for the first time could prove to be a joyous and happy occasion for Bruce. He had talked to a lady on the phone for a couple of weeks, and tonight they would meet at a restaurant near his house. He was fascinated by the charm and appeal of a potential romance. The meeting was okay, but the woman ended up being someone he just couldn't get next to, and it appeared that the same was true on her end as well. And since he had to work for several hours on New Year's Day, he would go home and spend the evening quietly watching television and listening to music. He really didn't have money for going out on the town anyhow.

He did have reflections of a lady he once knew named Cindy, whose birthday is New Year's Eve. He did phone her to leave a birthday message, and was surprised that the number he had for her was now still good. She wasn't at home, but left a message inviting her to go out sometime, saying that it's up to her what she wants to do.

Janice was wiped out from working and was in a quandary as to how to best spend the evening. Whether she chose to celebrate at home, attend a small party, or having been invited to a gala affair, she knows that she would expect to have a wonderful time mingling with other friendly folk. But before going out to celebrate, she would take time to ponder goals she hopes to achieve during the year ahead. These would involve cutting down on soda and junk food to get her in better health. And maybe do some more walking, as she lives in an area where this is possible.

Janice was not exempt from the need to go into work on New Year's Day, so she didn't really feel like dancing and having fun. She invited a gentleman friend of hers to come over for a spell. This was not an intimate friend, and this couldn't have happened anyway as the girls were home. At midnight they would make a toast and wish each other Happy New Year.

25

IT WAS A BOUNTIFUL holiday season for Janice. She was glad for the opportunity to spend New Year's Eve in the company of an older man named Derrek. While not one she would consider a full-time love, he at least is a well-respected man around her part of town, a refreshing change from some of the losers she had been involved with before. He even knows she often wishes she had never become involved with the fathers of her three girls even though she is glad she has the girls. She had high hopes for especially the relationship with James Duane, the father of the two oldest girls Krystal and Jamicia. She ended up losing him when she didn't provide him with a son. He does, at times, dote on the girls on the rare occasions when he sees them, such as during Christmas. Michael, the father of Serena, was also a bit of a deadbeat as well. He accepted an employment offer in Texas, and as a result won't really be around much to see her.

As this brand new year begins, romance and continuing on with the party would occupy most of her time and thoughts. Having to go in to work, she really would sleep walk through much of the day not being her usual somewhat bossy self. This was a starred day to ignore the daily routine and spend time having fun with loved ones. Obviously Janice had other things on her mind besides work. But toward the end of the time there she settled in and for a change actually seemed congenial. She didn't have to be so nice, but she was much to Bruce's amazement.

She was also dressed very nicely, and he paid her a compliment. In his own mind he guessed that if she had to be there, she might as well perk herself up. Janice, the one associated normally with thinking processes, now moved into quirky conversation. Bruce found this somewhat appealing, but figured it must be only a blip on the radar screen. He guessed that on the next day she'll be back to her rather stern self.

Janice was ready to leave work at the very first minute she could, and concentrate on her house, family and property. Having lost the loving feeling for the men who have crossed her path, she needed time to think. So she contacted her aunt, who was staying with the girls while she was at work, and asked if she could stay a while longer and said that she could. She would embark on a drive to the lake shore and park the car and just meditate for the hour or so she had until sundown.

For the next three weeks reminiscing about past events and sharing nostalgic memories can be a very pleasant pastime. Both Bruce and Janice would do this. Each in their own way, they would in their minds take a leisurely walk down memory lane and make the effort to revisit the past. Bruce would say that nobody but him could have experienced many of the things he has, both the good and not so good. He has many a question that remains unanswered, and may never be so.

And each in their own way, both Bruce and Janice would, once all the recollection and nostalgic dreaming was out of the way, then look forward to a wonderful future full of potential and opportunities. While Bruce would make it his priority to do the best job he can at his present job, it was now that he began to feel an attraction toward Janice. But he knew that he would have to break it to her gently if he ever got the nerve to really express this to her. As neither of them has written down their goals for the coming year, they would set aside time to do this today.

26

LIGHTNING NOW APPEARED TO be striking, and Bruce was feeling more fortunate than he had been in some time. A good blend of romance, luck, and ability would help him achieve his goals and satisfy his needs. Both Bruce and Janice were back on the job. Bruce especially felt that he should be extremely productive, and Janice even more so if putting in a few extra hours to stay on top of new developments. As a lead person for her department she considered this necessary. Seldom if ever did she bother to take lunch during the workday.

Janice was very well dressed this day and Bruce was really impressed. He wondered how she would be dressed come summer. Being in her presence inspired him. Energy would remain high and good fortune was on his side, helping him to feel as if for a change he would be able to be at the right place at the right time. Lots of compliments would begin coming Janice's way, and Bruce was apt to feel more generous than usual.

There was one coworker, whose name is Tim, whom she often referred to as her boyfriend. But this was all in fun, and there really was no relationship off-campus between them. He worked late afternoons and evenings, and there would on occasion be an overlapping of their schedules.

Through the years Janice saw a lot of party lights, and although not giving away too many details, she admits to having made mistakes she has learned from, and encourages those she works with to do the same. But for the most part she tries not to concentrate a lot on yesterday, being more concerned with today and tomorrow. But this confession piqued Bruce's interest, and privately he wondered if she was a real boogie baby at one point in her life. He didn't even know for sure as to if Janice had an actual boyfriend, but assumed that if she had, especially if it was serious, that it would have been discovered by this time. It seemed as if she was unattached.

One of Bruce's hobbies is writing song lyrics, but he really can't make music. At present he is getting ready to have a demo mode of one of his writings put to music. He has to pay for the production. Among his resolutions was that if he can afford to splurge on something he has wanted for ages but it wasn't under the Christmas tree, he would treat himself by making this purchase now. He had to pay in two payments, and was told that his demo should be ready by late March. This is something he has always wanted to do, but was always leery of all these dream merchants who promise a pot of gold but deliver nothing and often scam the unexpecting. He now awaits the finished product and hope it turns out well. Above all, he hopes that he will like it.

27

BRUCE WOULD, AS A creative person, attempt to be so in convincing himself that it's all right to have a liking for a coworker, even if it happens to be one who is in a position over him. After all, that was the case with his own parents. Janice hadn't really got to him yet to the point where he couldn't sleep at night, but that was soon to come. Adding a touch of individuality to his life would bring out his creative side. He had just self-published a fiction story and was working on another one in addition to several song lyrics. No music, however.

Although Janice has been quite stubborn about moving away from her down-at-the-heels neighborhood, she is beginning to think more seriously about making a change. She really doesn't want to expose her girls to the pathologies present around them. Friends and coworkers have told her that if she is on the hunt for a home, good progress can now be made as home prices have dropped over the last three months. Yet a part of her feels stuck.

The early days of the New Year are also an excellent time to assess the state of your overall health and well-being. As her diet currently doesn't pass scrutiny, and her fitness regime is a little on the slack side, Janice would consider what she can do to change this. She came up with a plan to cut down on junk food, eat healthier, and do more walking. Perhaps it was time for her to become reacquainted with the exercise bike languishing in the attic or the running shoes in the back of the closet. She totally forgot that bike was even there. The running shoes might not be broken back into until spring, as they don't do well during icy conditions.

Bruce has never been one for fad diets or other food regimens. He developed a bit of a bulge around the middle during his Lorraine days, as she fed him a lot. She was often after him to eat more fruits and veggies, which he has tried to do. He has a favorite candy and finds the thought of giving that up to be spooky.

He had dabbled a bit into an Internet dating site, and tentatively had plans to meet a woman at a local pizza place this evening, but was told to call her in advance. He had the premonition that social arrangements were likely to be disrupted or cancelled this evening. So he phoned the woman, whose name was Mary Lou, to confirm the arrangements. She wasn't at the phone so he left her a message.

After a time he figured he may not hear back. Now Janice was heavy on his mind, but he was up for meeting Mary Lou as a diversion. As he was eager to paint the town red, he needed to have some backup plans at the ready to avoid disappointment. But he also needed the willpower to avoid common pitfalls such as the urge to drink and drive. It's the end of the holiday period, and cops would be out in full force. Mary Lou never called, and no big night out occurred.

28

JANICE WAS NOT A beautiful woman, just average. But just one look at her would get Bruce's imagination stirring up loving thoughts. At first, he secretly hoped that she would take to him as well. He now felt as if love is in the air, and that his potential lover is residing in a cubicle nearly across from him, even though he knew that the chance of anything like that happening was slim to none for the sole reason of her position as his lead person. But he could still dream. And when he did he saw a vision of romance, fun, and frivolity, while also merging with the passionate side of his character. Although not as yet having the nerve to let her know, he really wanted Janice to be his girl, although she was more than two decades his junior and had three girls of her own. Feelings for her as an object of affection would intensify. He hoped that he would find that the opportunities for such a love affair would increase.

Part of the mystique in his mind, and what really got his heart jumping was learning that she once was quite a party girl and wondered if she still had some of that mindset embedded within. When one does a lot of reckless celebrating the chance of conception rises as a result, warning those not ready for parenthood to take extra precautions. She had mentioned that she was about 23 at the peak of her partying days, and that this was the age at which she had her first child. Although not really having the desire to be a parent himself. Bruce found this part of her past to be intriguing, and wanted to know more.

Now attempting to detach his mindset from these thoughts, he felt that working his way through household chores could be comforting. Not having a lot of living space didn't mean that he was free of things to do. He always seemed to end up with stacks of bills and other items coming in the mail, more than he knows what to do with.

The landlady he rents living space from is someone who has a green thumb, and spends a lot of time outside during the warm part of the year. Bruce himself kept a vegetable garden during his boarding school years. But the landlady does not have indoor plants, which he finds a bit surprising. It could be that she would need to pay so much extra attention to them. He has never asked, and has never fully considered having indoor plants himself.

At the time of his youth he was an athletic minded person who felt he could excel at a favorite sport. He had a desire to participate in little league baseball but got sent away to boarding school before ever getting the chance. Being stuck there during his formative years effectively robbed him of the opportunity to partake in sports, go to dances and meet and date girls, along with other normal teenage things. The only positive in his mind is that it made him ineligible to participate in the Vietnam War.

Janice had to make sure that her girls were well-prepared for the return to school following the two-week long winter break. She was glad to have had time over the period to spend with them, and that they have remained healthy and without disease. Krystal, the oldest, is looking forward to the return with anticipation, while the middle girl, Jamicia, is more ho-hum, and doesn't seem to be as good a student. Serena, just three, will start pre-school soon, but right now goes to a day care center while Janice is at work. She hopes that any and all matters involving her dear children will proceed smoothly.

29

A BUMPY ROAD WAS now in store for Bruce, as a number of upsets would prove challenging until later in the day, when life would finally settle down. At work he was dogged by thoughts of things he should have said to Janice but was too timid to do so. By the end of the afternoon he was so tired that when he arrived at home he promptly proceeded to take a nap, which is actually fairly common for him during the dark winter months.

With his unexplained fascination with Janice beginning to overtake him, he is at a cross roads at which time, unless he looked for solid facts amid the unrealistic attitude that permeates his daily life, he could set off on a wild-goose chase in his desire to go to Loveland. And largely unknown to him now the rumor mill would be rife with gossip and innuendo, but remained determined not to get too caught up in the web. At this point he truly believes that there is apt to be more fantasy than truth to what is being whispered in talk behind the scenes.

Experience in being a victim of fault finding has shown Bruce that the art of trying to live up to the expectations of other people will be an exercise in futility and should be avoided. For example Robin, the woman in the next cubicle, who will soon celebrate her 60th birthday, is one who will beg him to help her with a work issue when Janice is unable to, and yet can deliver snide remarks when she feels that a comment he makes isn't up to snuff in her view. For this reason he looks forward to Tuesday, when she is off as she works on Sundays.

Instead of concerning himself so much he does his best in aiming to consider his own potential and strives to achieve his own aims. This is why he tries to bat a thousand on performance every day, his hope being that he will eventually get hired and a tempting financial proposition could come out of the blue and be worth further investigation. Little did he know at this time what would be in store for him down the road?

30

THE FOLLOWING DAY JANICE came to work wearing a stunning blue dress which really caught Bruce's eye. She doesn't dress up for work that often, so he wondered to himself if she had a hot date that evening. As a child he learned all about heroes and villains from the comics and the television shows of the time. But these exist in the real world as well. While at first Bruce seemed to be a hero in the eyes of some workers and even Paula, the department supervisor, his crush on Janice is beginning to turn him into a villain due, interestingly, to an apparent outbreak of jealousy from other men in the company who may wish that they could be her buttercup rather than her being Bruce's.

Meanwhile Bruce finds it quite comforting to be in Janice's presence even though she can be subject to off moods from time to time. He is now finding himself eager to get up in the morning and head to work even on these dark, bitter cold mornings of midwinter.

Bruce thought what a wonderful world it would be if he could get a bit closer to Janice, feeling as though a sense of mutual harmony and support would provide peaceful, secure surroundings. Throughout the morning hours he felt as though there was nothing he could do to cut loose from these feelings. However, he would aim to complete challenging tasks before early afternoon, because if it was real busy Janice would not be as supportive later in the day. By now, his primary goal was to be able to keep her happy at all costs. At the same time, he hoped to be taken on by the company as a regular worker. He hoped that an offer he received could have merit and lead to a brighter financial future, providing he were to have calculated all the risks and read the fine print. He knows from having signed up with Cadence and the other staffing agencies he had signed up with that there is a vast amount of paperwork and legalese to sign off on before accepting a job offer—far more than in the days when he first began working.

For love of Janice he would soar to new heights. He now looked so forward to those occasional times when at the close of the day they could talk for a few minutes about things not work related. He hoped that these chats, which did not occur every day, would bring them at least a *little bit closer*. An emotional dialogue was unlikely to be about the actual subject under discussion but instead be a lot deeper, at least in his mind.

Others on the staff, however, would sense something less than desirable, at least in their eyes. They would now make the very best effort, feeling the need to listen, tune in and do some intense digging to find the root of the problem and then resolve it.

31

BRUCE WOULD BE DOGGONE if he knew of the thorny atmosphere which now existed behind the scenes. In order to make his feelings toward Janice less obvious he would now do his best to maintain a down-to-earth approach with all workplace dealings or he might be confronted with larger issues in the near future.

Away from the job it was important to astutely evaluate his struggling finances. He lives quite simply and has never concerned himself with material investments outside of a car. Things such as stocks, bonds and real estate investing never interested him much. He did, however, convert an account from a previous employer into a standard IRA to rein in further value erosion which had begun to take hold. His parents had left him a trust from which he receives disbursements, but it's one of those where the terms cannot be changed once the creator is deceased. He has thought about at least moving the trust over to his own bank so he would have everything in one location, but for now has chosen to keep the relationship with his current trust advisor.

On this work day Janice was sharply dressed in a stunning purple and white outfit, but tried not to notice too strongly. Professional and career concerns are at this time likely to test his resolve, and she would probably need to stand her ground in order to make headway. There has been some drift toward the idea that she may have some attraction to Bruce as well, but something is telling her that she needs to stifle it.

A member of her staff will soon be moving on to other things. Little by little she is making plans for her departure. But plans for a special party or other function in her honor would run into problems. As time was on her side, she now felt it would be wise to leave decision making in this regard until tomorrow. She is aware that pleasing all of the people all of the time is an impossibility. Besides, she has three girls; therefore there is a real good possibility someone at home could be demanding more than she has to give.

32

THE ONE PARTICULAR THING which has dogged Bruce for his entire life was his nature to be impulsive. This trait has landed him in trouble a few times, and in the back of his mind he is well aware that it could happen again. This would be another day on which to act on important tasks in the morning before issues begin to make life more difficult. Spontaneity may be in order but he always needs to beware of impulsiveness, which could lead him into trouble. By now it was no secret that he liked being around Janice, and he also got a hint that she enjoyed being in his company as well. She would often remark that Bruce had a way with words. For him, her presence was all he would need to get by in what otherwise might be a rather mundane job—one he might not consider keeping if more jobs were available.

This evening he had no particular place to go. To help curb restlessness, he would engage in pursuits that are different, unusual, and exciting as well as productive. He did have a flair for writing.

A creative project could now benefit from original, unique ideas. On this night he would rework a song lyric he came up with some years back in hopes that he could soon have it set to music and then distribute it. He took Janice's comments to heart, hoping this can inspire him. He has long dreamed of being one who could write or lecture for a living.

Indeed he does feel he should find that a flair for words could keep the audience stimulated and entranced.

He was in the middle of a project when he received a call from Laura. She is usually not spontaneous, preferring to have things planned in advance. But on this occasion she offered to pay for a meal out. As it was, going out with her for a scrumptious dinner of cuisine from another country would be the highlight of his day. Yet she is not one whom he feels really in love with. He feels himself now falling for Janice, but knows it would be a lost cause because of her position. He prays that somehow the Lord will have mercy on his soul.

33

BRUCE'S EMOTIONAL STATE WAS now in a fragile condition, similar to which he had not seen for about ten years. By coincidence, that time it was a situation somewhat similar to this one. A lady named Mary whom he worked with for just one week swept him up in a very similar situation to this one. And he had a somewhat casual girlfriend, Alice, during that time frame. A few years later he did run into Mary by chance. They talked briefly, but by then any sort of obsession which may have existed had vanished. On the particular day of this encounter he had a big date with a woman named Eleanor with whom he had gotten acquainted with through the personal ads. They planned to go out for dinner and a movie.

Feelings would now run high for him as the infatuation over Janice comes to the full in the course of caring for a sometimes cranky woman. He desires to do whatever he can to keep the sunny side of her visible—that way he will enjoy his time there.

On Janice's side of the ledger an ending was foreseen in regard to a domestic and often emotional matter, and change to the family unit or home life was a distinct possibility. Her aunt had informed her that her father, whom she had been estranged from for years, was coming to live with her. Since he is seriously ill, her aunt may need Janice to occasionally run errands for him. She would need to remind her emphatically that not only is she a career woman but also a single mother. She will do what she can along this line but can't be at her aunt's constant beck and call.

A man known as John Henry, one a few years her junior at 29 has been an on-again, off-again love encounter over the past few years. He is someone of questionable character, and Janice is dubious of him being around her girls. It's not that he is a pervert by any means, but he is still not a good role model. Additionally, she has moved on to a less hedonistic and more focused lifestyle in the years since this particular relationship began. Still, he is reluctant to take no for an answer.

At one point Janice was concerned that he might have gotten her pregnant. This was around the time of the Full Moon, and somehow she knew that babies often make an appearance at Full Moon. She went round and round about this, and finally decided she would get tested. As she had already had three deliveries in her life she wasn't sure how her body would handle a fourth. But fortunately the tests were negative. She swears she is through making babies.

For her children study and research would proceed smoothly. Both of the oldest girls were now involved in special projects at school, and she would now need to make time in her schedule to provide assistance wherever she could in the hope that their ability to be able to concentrate on intellectual pursuits will be easier. She knows that some interesting facts may be uncovered in the process. On this evening she would make a spaghetti dinner for the girls and her and allow plenty of quality time in which to discuss these concerns.

It was a crisp, cold winter day, and while shopping for dinner she also would spend a little time browsing in a bookstore searching for a good mystery novel which could appeal as she would prefer to stay in rather than socializing this evening.

34

FAR FROM THE RECKLESS spirit of earlier times, Janice was now in a cautious mode. She has the hunch that Bruce is eating his heart out over her, but is uncertain as to how she is going to deal with it. She has enough to contend with in other areas of her life, and certainly hopes that his goal was not marriage, what with the vast age difference and the task of raising her three girls. He did once mention to her casually that his own parents had met each other at work.

Forward planning would be needed involving her girls' academic studies, and also vocational training for herself, as she may be moving into a new position before long. An overseas journey can also be beneficial. A long-time ago a friend of hers invited her to fly down to Trinidad "sometime"-and the idea of sipping piña coladas on a secluded beach does sound appealing. As she has plenty of vacation accumulated, she should now look into travel destinations that would provide relaxation or an exciting vacation.

Changes at home and issues with a sibling would become more prominent now that communication between her two oldest girls has moved into a state of jealous motions between them. Krystal has now emerged as the most intelligent, which is common among the first born. This has left Jamicia a bit uncertain about her place in the world. Janice herself has a brother who lives several miles away. Their relationship moved into retrograde some time back and she now owed him a visit.

Her away from work priorities are now clearly in her family and home sector, far away from the party lights of her younger days. She may need to be available to help her father, who has been going through a difficult time with his health. But because of her other responsibilities as a worker and a parent she cannot allow this to chain her down exclusively. She also has considered a move, but as the market is down she knows this is not a good time to sign a lease or buy a new home.

Although normally not a believer in such things, on a whim Janice chose to get a reading from a local psychic, who saw that from now until February 1 household items may malfunction or break and travel plans may be disrupted. While she has no plans for leisure travel between now and then, she is concerned about what might happen with her long working commute. Sure enough, one morning shortly thereafter a major wreck occurred on her way to work. As a result, she was close to two hours late, and while she did reach out by cell phone to those she needed to inform, the rank and file people in her area did not know, and Bruce in particular wondered if she was in a wreck. He expressed this concern briefly to Robin, who told him that he was just like her, being an obsessive worry wart. They were relieved when she did walk in and she told everybody the story of the massive traffic jam she had to endure on this hazy winter morning.

Somewhat milder weather combined with the snow cover produced a dense fog, one car didn't see another and they collided right in the midst of the morning rush. Now that Janice arrived safely the department could settle into the day's tasks objectively. All this would make a sea cruise or some other kind of exotic vacation more inviting than ever to Janice.

35

BRUCE FOR MUCH OF his life was attracted to stylish women, as he considered his mother to be. But yet his most outstanding love of recent years, Lorraine, was quite the contrary. She was heavy set and a very casual dresser. Yet they were perfect for each other in a number of ways. When he would reveal some of the more disturbing points of his past he would sometimes begin to break down, and she would respond that it was, well, all right.

Today an efficient, practical mood would assist him as he was involved in trying to make the best impression possible so that Janice would see what he could do. The possibility of negotiating or closing a deal for a permanent position was on his mind too. Little did he know at this time about the monkey wrench plot working against him behind the scenes where many who seemed to be friendly toward him upfront would do whatever they could to keep him and Janice from ever getting closer.

For her part, Janice began getting extra requests for special projects and favors. Following the ordeal of the crash related delay; she would rise and shine a little earlier this morning, because another time may come when she may be plagued by delays at home or to experience problems with transportation. She has a twelve year-old car she uses for the commute, and so far she has been lucky that it has served her well.

It's not unusual right now for Bruce and Janice to banter a bit during the not so busy points in the day. He would make every effort to put his best foot forward and other people would be bound to notice. And as his lead person he felt that Janice was the main one he needed to impress. Being anywhere near Janice made Bruce feel young and lively. He was hoping they could at least get together away from the office. He now guessed that as long as he advanced with humility, singing his own praises could help him move another rung up the ladder.

Activities involving family members would be pleasant for Janice, and on her way home she would stop to pick up a movie she thought the girls would enjoy. On this cold night she was seeking home entertainment. Her oldest child now seemed to have the magic touch when it came to some of her school projects. Over dinner this evening she would tell Krystal that one day taking a creative writing course or an art class could bring out her innovative style. And in fact a class trip to the well-known art museum was coming up, and Janice would need to sign the permission slip so Krystal could go. That morning she would take time before work to wait at the bus stop to see her board. They would then connect to the subway for the ride into the museum. At this point it made her beam with pride that she has quite a gifted daughter. She knows it won't be easy, but reflections on her own life make her want Krystal to do better than she herself has done.

36

AS MUCH AS HE felt that being in Janice's company was akin to being in heaven, Bruce was unaware of the tricky circumstances behind the scenes. For certain he was feeling as though it was a groovy kind of scenario, but folks yet unbeknownst to him were plotting as to how to negate any potential affair between them. And yet Bruce didn't really consider a work environment where three shifts run an ideal situation. He would have preferred a one-shift, Monday thru Friday situation. That is his current schedule but knows it could change on a moment's notice. But in a down economy he felt that he had better hold on to what he's got.

Bruce by now has made no secret of how he enjoys bantering back and for with Janice during slower periods when possible. He gets an impression of being swept away on some sort of a magic carpet ride. But this isn't going to be the easiest of days for either of them and he will soon be well aware of that.

This was to be no lazy day. Both Bruce and Janice, each in their own way, would feel as if there is no letup from routine chores, but as the department lead, Janice would also need to know when to delegate or say no to additional work which was handed to her. With her temperament fragile at times, she would need to as best she can ignore insensitive comments from a colleague or boss. They know that she should be doing a good job handling her duties, and they may just be venting their own frustrations rather than constructive criticism.

While she also on occasion does this with Bruce, he has nevertheless become infatuated enough with her that he is now willing to do things any way she wants them, and has on occasion volunteered for some of the more mundane tasks when the necessities were caught up with, which soon will be less often as a new account was on the way. Just for her Bruce was determined to find ways to be able to do the work at hand just a little bit better.

With all this in mind, Bruce vowed to do his best not to get upset if work takes a little longer than expected to complete. So far he has not developed the nerve to reveal his attraction to Janice, but it has become obvious that some certain things he has done has led others to believe it is indeed true. In casual conversation he learned that Janice wishes to concentrate on reestablishing ties with a friend as she has been a little neglectful in this area lately. He did not know if this wish referred to another female friend or one who was male. He knew she was single, and that meant that the fathers of her girls did not provide her with an everlasting love. She usually didn't reveal too much about her personal life at work, but to himself he now wondered if the fathers of the girls were natural wanderers, the type one might encounter in the wild partying scene she admittedly was once a part of. Anyway, he began to wonder secretly whether he would love the way she loves, hoping one day to get the chance to find out.

Folks behind the scenes were by now full of suspicion. But as time goes by the plot would thicken. As Bruce was well aware, there were sometimes obnoxious attitudes toward any sort of workplace liaison. Therefore, he might need to make it clear to a coworker or friend that offering any kind of support or sympathy is not a signal for romance. He was searching every which way for ideas on how to keep his admiration for Janice under wraps as much as possible, but knows success would be subdued at best.

37

A MIXED BAG WOULD await Bruce on the following day, and he would feel he was riding the waves between high and low surf. A flurry of activity would have him on his toes, but he would at the same time be feeling a little down in the dumps. Doubtful that his feeling for Janice could be reciprocated, his mind turned to thoughts of Lorraine, the woman he could have been happy together with were it not for his stubborn desire to retain more independence than she could have been comfortable with. Now and then he would contemplate the idea of asking her to return, vowing that he would pay her back with interest as far as love and devotion are concerned. He does not now have nearly the desire for wanderlust that he still did at the time when they were together. Once he comes to he returns to thoughts of trying to make a living as a writer of novels and song lyrics in the hope that it could provide adequate escape from the vagaries of the corporate world as it now is.

He has written one book and in fact gave Janice a copy of it to read. And he has also on occasion offered to stay a bit past normal quitting time at the job, also uncharacteristic of him unless formally mandated. Often miffed by those he feels are too busy to get out to socialize, he might as well try to become too busy himself. Yet he is clearly unhappy with this whole "I don't have time" syndrome which has invaded the culture. Yet he now seldom thinks about much else besides Janice when he doesn't have to. If he could just get close to her, even if not permanently, that'll be the day he feels the mission has been accomplished. Not that he is looking for the proverbial one-night stand, but if nothing develops further his curiosity will at least have been satisfied. For his entire life he has found the game of love to be strange—one in which many say they want a relationship yet not really mean it. He would attend singles activities and dances with usually less than the desired results.

As Bruce has been overdoing, tiredness could now cause negative thoughts, including the idea that he doesn't have anything since he doesn't yet have Janice as an important piece of his life. In self-therapy he'd try to dwell on all the positives that are occurring in his life, such as having a job to go to when there are now so many who do not. This he hopes would help him to better cope with the sounds of silence while he is home.

For Janice, meanwhile, good news in the form of an overdue bonus or pay raise would cheer her up. This would serve to save the day as she had overspent for the recent holidays and is now facing large credit card debt. On her off-work time a family member and a friend would argue, and she would find herself caught in the middle. If possible she would try to not take sides; the hard feelings should eventually blow over. But circumstances surrounding the argument would make it easier said than done not to get into a tether over this.

Janice now can't help herself when it comes to the mixed bag involving Bruce. She does feel a spiritual connection toward him yet feels that because of her position nothing could happen there. At the same time this man of questionable character wants to get back with her. A friend of hers, a woman named Jennifer Johnson, is convinced that he would lead her down the wrong path and as a sideline could even put her career in jeopardy by leading her back into the round-the-clock party scene. But in the end Jennifer would tell Janice that she needed to leave it up to her what she should do, but hopes that she would make the wise move and not do it.

38

IF JANICE REALLY WAS ready for love following a long hiatus, she was, for the most part, being evasive as far as admitting to it was concerned. Her off-duty concern was projects her girls are involved in. Krystal and Jamicia have taken to selling some baked goods at a local sale to raise funds for some after school programs for underprivileged children. They even told their mom that raising money for a good cause should be a breeze. They would just put on a persuasive face and get started. But the siblings did argue quite a bit as to who should sell the most to which people. Although Janice is not one to back away from confrontation, she wouldn't be in the mood for petty disputes, and she told them so, saying that if they wished to do the project there would have to be peace with each other.

Her car would get a good workout as she runs errands and then heads off on a short business trip, as she would need to visit a technology center in order to learn a new program being installed at her work station.

In order that she can ensure that this will all run smoothly, she would set up an appointment to make sure that regular maintenance work gets done to avoid an annoying breakdown or mechanical problem.

Her hopes for a peaceful evening would be dashed. A power struggle involving her two oldest girls would come to a crescendo. The siblings once again began arguing over whose sales were rightfully whose at the sale. Janice would not let this shake her up, and when the donnybrook occurred this evening she laid down the law and told them they cannot take on any more such ventures until and unless they could make peace. Unless she took such action who knows what could develop later on. An early bedtime for Jamicia and time alone on the computer for Krystal, who needed to turn in a class assignment, would be the scenario she would mandate in order to hope this could keep this argument and discord from erupting. In doing so she would still assure both girls that she loves them and wants the best for them.

39

IT WOULD BE A disconcerting day for Janice, with escapist stars blazing in today's skies. She really wasn't feeling up to par, and it was a wonder that she made it through the day at work. It may have been fortunate that her superior Paula was off this day, as she would experience a distinct lack of interest for routine tasks, and as a result felt that it would be wise to leave strenuous chores until next week. She would not push herself even if she did have a hectic schedule. Fortunately for her the load was light as she was in no state to do more than the bare necessities. It was indeed a rare day for this department lead who under normal conditions can be a rather stern taskmaster. She is a believer that more will be accomplished and fewer errors will be made if one proceeds at a steady pace rather than rushing through the activity. As lead it is her job to call the operators to account when errors are made, and last week she had to inform Bruce about a few of his own.

An unsettling brew was being stewed behind the surface, however. Sheila, one of the main office coordinators, has been briefed of Bruce's apparent interest in Janice. An underlying issue could resurface, but for now Sheila would need a little more time to decide how she will proceed with things. She has no direct authority on issues, but to herself she feels it is a wonder that Bruce hasn't been brought down yet.

But the obvious attraction has taken some toll on Bruce physically, and an acquaintance was telling him that his run-down state with lack of sleep was signaling to him that it is time for him to restore some balance in his daily routine, and that he should consider scheduling a meditation retreat or investigating various relaxation techniques. And yet his financial situation resulting from being unable to work for some sixteen weeks following the fall he suffered less than a year ago forced him to be careful about making decisions including how to express his sudden feeling for Janice.

40

WHILE BRUCE'S ACQUAINTANCE WAS trying to be helpful, the result still was yet another sleepless night. Although quite drained, mild restlessness would find him up and about early today. He would make every attempt to apply this energy constructively by focusing on weekend chores and personal activities as soon as he would rise, before vim and vitality fade. With the streets and sidewalks icy from recent weather conditions he would need to take extra care in order to avoid slipping and sliding while outside. The public library is only a few blocks away and he often walks there. Not wanting to go through another fall, he would make sure to wear boots with good footing during rough winter weather.

With Janice first and foremost on his mind he would need to avoid being demanding toward those around him both at and away from the workplace. He feels that she would display a "catch me if you can" attitude if she really knew that he was really attracted toward her.

Try as he may, he had a hard time trying to not allow a sense of discord to upset weekend plans. Never one to seek out the in crowd, Bruce preferred to socialize with everyday people which he often feels there are fewer of these days. He has been known to go round and round with people in discussions of how he feels things ought to be, and is highly dismayed with all the political correctness now in vogue. In recent times few women have crossed his path whom he felt could really rock his soul, but now feels as if Janice is the one who could do it. As a coincidence, or maybe not, that was also the name of his very first girlfriend during first grade. He had also met another girl with that name at a social gathering but left her behind when another lady came up and began talking. He later regretted this, and once wrote a song lyric about it which he now would revise and recycle, and put it to the front of the list for having it demoed to music.

For most of his life Bruce has been unlucky in love and has often been afraid to get seriously involved, not knowing if he would still be loved come tomorrow. Even Laura, his closest female companion these days, is in many ways a poor match for him because she is a staunch early morning person, while he relished the nighttime. When he learned that Janice was once a party girl was when he developed the attraction full tilt. He figured that she could be one with whom he could go out and dance and have fun with at night, which Laura is not. But yet he has refused to quit being the great pretender here. Sooner or later he is going to have to tell her that even though they have been intimate on occasion, they really aren't a good match. He doesn't really want to bring her down, but he feels as if she does know the truth. Lorraine, the woman he could have married, was not a big nightlife person either. However he now feels there will never be another one like her.

Janice has showed Bruce that there are some lively spirited people out there, which he had begun to doubt. But he has a lot of misgivings about how to go about handling this. As he has been keeping a confidence and holding back personal information, he could be comforted by making a disclosure. But what if it totally backfires on him? The thought of this happening would keep him from coming clean for a time yet. After all she's a woman, and he knows all too well how fickle they can be.

With his vitality having faded as evening set in, he was unsure as to how he wished to spend the time. Resting at home, a relaxing massage, or going to the movies could be the perfect way to unwind from the stresses of the working week. The former choice would win, although he had the urge to partake in some nightlife. But after learning of police roadblocks he knew it would be best to leave the car at home if heading out for a heavy social night, especially if one will be drinking. He chose staying in.

41

AFTER A QUIET NIGHT at home with adequate sleep for a change, some favorable conditions would set in. Unlike yesterday, Bruce would be eager to get out and about and to be noticed by other people. With the messenger in his head smiling with a luck-bearing attitude, he was now more than ready to thank this invisible source of attitude adjustment. As the condition he was apparently born with has made it difficult for him to fit into this society, he has often been forced to create his own fun, for better or worse. Gaining knowledge over time has helped somewhat, and he actually did have his share of good times in the more liberal social environment of earlier times. But he is quite bothered and bewildered by all of today's political correctness. Having been confined to boarding school in his formative years robbed him of much of the chance to participate in taking a girl to an amusement park and many other fun things that young girls and boys did in those more innocent times.

For Janice all the strains of a responsible corporate position were now taking their toll. In her dreamy states arranging an overseas vacation could be a positive way to broaden her horizons. But for now the responsibility of raising three girls in addition to limited finances keeps these thoughts parked right where they are—in her dreams.

Her responsibilities as a lead person contain a dynamic where it is essential to focus on all details, both minor and major. And she passes this piece of advice along to all those in her department. Plans for a reunion party with a couple of long ago friends would occupy her free time and make excellent use of her natural organizing skills, especially as she will be hosting the celebration. At the same time she has advertised some things for sale. As a result the phone at her home is apt to ring with frequency with interested buyers eager to make a deal. At least that is what she hopes, since folks would pay higher prices at retail.

42

IMPORTANT TIMES WERE AHEAD for Janice both on and off the job. With community spirit now high, this would be a great time for her to meet and establish ties with new neighbors. She now joins Krystal, Jamicia, Serena and her neighbors' children in a mutual get-together, and will have various activities over the next four weeks. This would provide an excellent chance to spend more time with her immediate and extended family members, renewing bonds with the older generation and playing with children. She would also plan an inexpensive outing or gathering so that she would share joy and create happy memories. She also would run into a former flame that happened to walk by. A man who at one time would really send her, she would now be content with just a platonic friendship. Then there is also the infatuation Bruce seems to have for her, whom she is unsure how to handle. Her feelings on this are mixed, as while her job position stands in the way she still is intrigued on some fronts.

This could also be a good time for Janice to improve living conditions by redecorating or relocating. For the former she would invite some input from her daughters. After all, it will also be their home until they are adults. She enjoys the girls very much, but there are times when she wishes she were free from all the responsibility, which is something every parent experiences at some time. But she tends to turn pale when she thinks about the time when they begin leaving the family nest for the first time.

The latter is a mixed bag, as ties to her grandmother and aunt, and now also her ailing father, keep her tied to the area even though she would like to be able to get the girls away from this rather raunchy neighborhood. It would be a good thing if more progress could clean up the area, and not long ago Janice signed a petition to get a pinball parlor where a very unsavory crowd hung out and caused numerous problems closed down.

43

FRUITFUL TIMES CONTINUED FOR Janice. Buying an outfit for a special dinner party she would be hosting for her friends would boost her self-esteem and confidence even though she felt foolish to spend as much on it as she did. But, she reasoned, this is to be a big happening—the kind of which only occurs once in a blue moon. While finances have been a problem, she could now look forward to better times. News of both a pay raise and a large refund on a defective purchase would put a smile on her face.

Since a couple of days remained before the big occasion, she would opt to remain at home in her spare leisure time this evening and would enjoy sorting through photos and creating an album of family memories and treasures. Among these was an old item which still unbeknownst to her could be more valuable than envisioned. So before putting an heirloom up for sale, she would need to have someone reliable and knowledgeable value it. She would search for a suitable person to do so.

There was a bright moon out tonight, so Janice and Jamicia went for a walk around their area. The neighborhood really isn't that great, and therefore the only time she walks at night with any of her girls is when the moon is shining bright. She is glad all over that she has them even though her relations with their fathers haven't been great. Krystal chose to stay in and keep an eye on Serena as she had things to do for a school project. For her mental stamina is high, assisting in formulating unique ideas and artistic themes. She is truly gifted, having developed an interest in dramatics as well. There is a good chance that once she reaches high school she could be in a school class production. Like any good parent, Janice hopes all the girls will have a life better than hers. Above all she hopes that they will make better personal choices than she did in her youth, and that they will be able to raise their children within a stable marriage, something she was unfortunate in.

44

BRUCE WOULD TRY HIS best to be reassuring that everything will turn out for the best and not let his feelings towards Janice ruin her career potential. Right now he is going to the job each day with the confidence that something that he feels is essential for his peace of mind or prestige would turn out well. But his desire to do whatever it takes to please her and keep her calm has by now sparked rumors that he is literally trying to be her puppet. If ever confronted he would no doubt deny it. But he was aware of the other side of her that he did not care for and wanted to keep that side from resurfacing. He would attempt to be the pied piper leading her to some promised land in order to keep this from happening. But never has he been what some refer to as an ass-kisser. Yet that is the impression that many there have developed. Robin, the woman at the next terminal, is morbid with fear that he is stepping on her ability to be able to advance or even remain on the job.

A stumbling pattern has persisted for Bruce where love life is concerned, and once broke up a same-sex friendship when he developed an interest in the girl of his best friend. This awkward situation led him away from developing close friendships and chose, for the most part, to go his own way, for better or worse. Yet another awkward happening would occur several years later when he was seduced by a crazy woman named Mary. She was a recovered alcoholic who had once been married to another alcoholic. He was introduced to her by his supervisor at the hospital he once worked at. He was also a recovered alcoholic and had invited him to attend an open AA meeting where he could witness the process. Bruce obtained Mary's phone number, but at the time she had no interest in dating him. But on a trip home after moving away, the former supervisor told him that Mary wanted to talk to him. She wanted to make amends for having rejected him years back. Little did he know what he was in for.

She seduced him hot and heavy. Mary had a crazy attitude and wanted him to move in with her right away. Although yesterday's gone, the memory of this harrowing experience still crosses his mind, and in some ways has affected his life ever since. He hopes to never have to experience anything like it again.

Janice would now take a couple of days off as she is in the middle of a home improvement project. She did not bother to inform the crew that she would be off. By now it was apparent that Bruce was finding her irresistible, and he asked Paula where she was, and it was only then that he learned that she was off, expressing surprise that she didn't inform them all. Although not a truly beautiful woman, he obviously had reached the point where it was difficult for him to take his eyes off of her when she was around. He would try to be as coy about this as he could, but by now the infatuation was quite deep.

On the project Janice was likely to find success through the result of applied effort. She was lucky enough to receive timely assistance from someone who is handy with his hands. And it was a former flame that is now happily married to someone else but at one time had her shaking all over. Before the work collaboration began she would know that they loved each other no more and that the relationship would consist only of him applying his skill set to the project at hand. The finished project would meet her expectations, and then she could begin enjoying improved living comfort. Her working partner knew that time was tight and that she would need to return to work, and was grateful of his acknowledgment of that. The purpose was twofold as the improvements would increase the home's value. A real estate purchase was not recommended until the market moves forward. However, this would be a good time to check out what property could be obtained for the money that she would intend to invest should she decide on a move.

45

A SURPRISING DEVELOPMENT WOULD make Bruce feel as if he had an angel on his shoulder. He was lucky to be able to even get a job as sparse as the market is at this time. Paula, the department supervisor above Janice, had given him a vote of confidence, saying that he was one of the best workers she had. Little did she know at this time that the classic 1960's song about one being the loneliest number would soon resonate as once the plot against him thickened that she would be standing alone and would be unable to continue to support him and save his job. And both Bruce and Paula, each in their own way, would have nowhere to run. As instructions were given by those higher up in the facility she would be unable to stop them from bringing him down. But for now things still seemed rosy. There was a town hall style meeting held this morning at which it was stated that new business was coming and would no doubt require some expansion of staff.

Although coming close a couple of times, Bruce has never been married. After spending his formative years in boarding schools he made up for lost time, determined to do so. He preached that variety is the spice of life, and for sure wouldn't be happy unless there was plenty of diversity in his daily environment and also in his love life. He joined singles clubs, attended dances, and answered newspaper personals ads. But after suffering a fall last year he reached the point where he felt that it doesn't matter anymore, and was now content to live a more low-key existence.

Then this was due largely to his inability to find work following the fall. Now that it was assumed that he would be working for the long term this was a time when he would be likely to come up with new ideas, dream up a novel scheme, or achieve a long-awaited breakthrough. The latter of this trio no doubt applied to Janice, who by now was one he felt he could fly to the moon with.

After having a staid social life outside his occasional dates with Laura, Bruce was ready for something different. Therefore he was likely by now to experience the urge to date someone who is very different from his usual romantic partner and was bound to desire to have some exciting but short-lived fun and romance. Janice seemed to fit this scenario on all counts. He knew there would be no possibility for a long-term situation, but a chance to go party with her would be nice to say the least. That is why he wanted to do what he could to keep her from coming undone, as she sometimes did when under considerable stress. He did want to make her his, if only for a short while or even in fantasy. He would also be inclined to do something unusual with his cash, but would need to guard against an overly impulsive attitude, which is not his strong suit. Neither does he possess the knack for good timing. And as a result he might later regret impetuous behavior and have to pay the price for it.

46

NOT ONLY DID BRUCE now possess a buoyant attitude when around Janice, but by now the workers around him sensed how he felt, which was that she is an extremely interesting woman. He has the confidence and energy needed to make positive changes, so he would concentrate on firming up plans that can help him move toward his goals. Overcoming obstacles was his real strength, and he has proven it before, despite some unlucky streaks. However there were some rumors circulating that Janice may soon be transferring to a new department where he would no longer be working with her. His reaction to this was one of dread. He was hoping that developments that come through communications or news from a distance could help with current aims. If there was a silver lining in this, he thought, it could in fact be easier to have a relationship with her if they were not in the same department, especially as she would no longer be his lead. But even he wondered if his attitude on this was too Pollyanna-like. He tried not to think about it.

Although a practical mood now prevails, Bruce still would feel a little agitated. To relieve this, he would keep on the move. He would take some short trips for pleasure during his off hours. Foremost on his mind was trying to plot a way in which to get closer to Janice. He considered writing a note and craft it the best way to get it signed, sealed and delivered to her. But for sure the gossip mill would be working overtime if he did so. As much as she had him reeling and rocking he still needed to use some caution. So he would write his note and keep it in the pouch where he keeps personal notes in until the right opportunity presented itself if indeed it ever did. Somehow he had developed the notion that she had acquired a loving feeling for him as well, or at least a personal attraction. He wanted to do what he could to at least maintain the current level of contact if not strengthen it. At this point he still had no idea that the loving feeling on her end would be lost, if in fact there ever was one.

Janice was also doing things behind the scenes. Short trips for business purposes may be more educational than profitable right now, but they were out of necessity as she is going into a new part-time venture with an old friend of hers. She can't voice her choice too strongly, however, as she doesn't wish to leave her present job right now. However, this is likely to change if she were to keep adding contacts to her network database.

At times she feels as if the customers aren't getting the level of service they deserve, and has expressed these thoughts out loud. And although often frustrated by some of the politics involved in any workplace scenario, she feels that her opinions are quite important, so she won't hesitate to express them and let other people know what is on her mind.

47

AS BRUCE STILL DIDN'T have Janice as an official part of his life, an unsteady aura lurked within him as he awoke to the rising sun. An abundance of pesky patterns would form today, but it was to be a case of positive and negative influences canceling each other out. He would expect a reasonable day despite life's ups and downs. Keeping on an even keel with love, romance, and monetary affairs is never easy and now is made even harder as sultry feelings toward Janice challenge the restrictive workplace environment made even more so by some of the edicts which have come down in recent years. Time after time he has failed to make peace within himself over this dilemma. Feelings now are apt to run hot and cold, so he would be best served to postpone any major decisions until emotions settle down and matters become a little clearer. But until that happens he would literally go round the roses with the "should I or shouldn't I" conundrum as far as taking action on officially expressing his attraction for Janice.

Janice also had a conundrum of her own. A couple of her friends wanted to get together, but were as yet undecided as to what to do. They thought about going into town but had heard that some rough weather could be on the way. She gave them the option of coming to her house for some food and frolic. She would get her aunt to watch the girls so they would have the house to themselves. One of the friends, Michelle, really wants to go clubbing because her birthday is the following day. But she said she would go along with what the others decided.

By nightfall the predicted storm had not yet arrived. And no decision had yet been reached regarding the evening's activity. Michelle and Janice shared a few laughs by phone in regards to one Halloween party where she went disguised as the devil, complete with horns. She said she knew a place where they could go. But for sure social plans that involve close friends should provide fun whether they were relaxing at home or enjoying the bright lights of the city.

48

THE LADIES ENDED UP going to the place Michelle had suggested. They had a great time and had no problems getting home as the predicted storm did not materialize in their area. An easygoing day was in store for Janice, although some of yesterday's influence would continue today. As a result, it would be wise to avoid risks and gambling, the latter of which she confines to the occasional lottery ticket. She may on occasion wish to be rescued from some things, but gambling would not be among them. She has heard a few horror stories in regards to those who fell into that hole. Energy would be a little under par, making this a morning to enjoy the comfort of her own bed for a little longer than usual. The girls were with her aunt, and she agreed to keep them until mid-afternoon. When she does go to pick them up she may take them to the mall for a treat. Since one of them will need new shoes, it would be the perfect time to go.

Janice's popularity now is rising, and her social calendar would now be full although at times she might prefer the opposite. Being a working career woman, a single parent plus having an active social life can end up being a triple crown of exhaustion. A man she once dated has asked her to meet him at the bus stop this evening. They had a falling out, and she still recalls the things they said when they parted company. Not being sure that anything could redevelop, she nevertheless agreed to meet to see if they could at least make peace.

Just the other day she had told Bruce that as a single person he should make the effort to go out and meet and greet a number of potential choices and one day he may be in luck. He has dabbled in an Internet dating site and has met a couple of ladies but no real sparks. But tonight he will take a long hot bath and then go out to a singles function he heard about. He has for the most part given up on those things in the last couple of years.

Bruce found a social occasion he did attend delightful, and he actually met one lady he found to be interesting although he isn't sure they will date. Her name was Jeannie, and they spent time playing board games which were available at the gathering. It was a fun way to meld together as a unit, and could be a start in rebuilding his social calendar which has been nearly empty over the past year.

49

IT WAS TO BE a renewing period for Janice and the dynamic this morning would accentuate her home and family sector. This means that over the next two weeks implementing home improvements or making plans to move should proceed smoothly. On the latter she is in a quandary as while she would like for the girls to grow up in a better neighborhood, she also has strong family ties that want to keep her grounded where she is at. She has heard that interest rates are down, making this also a great period for those seeking to buy a home to begin the search for that dream property. However, she wouldn't want to sign on the dotted line until her career life moves forward, which should happen late in February as she assumes her new position at her current workplace in addition to helping out her friend Brenda in the beauty supply business. She would have to make sure she can meet what would no doubt be a hefty mortgage payment every month or it would be for naught.

She wasn't really prepared for the happy news, but was told that another friend of hers had become engaged to be married. The couple had met last summer while walking in the rain to an art gallery and the marriage will take place during the coming summer. They made a date to meet for lunch at twelve-thirty this Saturday at a retro diner inside a nearby shopping mall. She will be glad to partake in this blessed event despite her occasional wistfulness at not having a lover of her own at present.

Tonight for a change she would choose to spend quality time with loved ones. At the same time Bruce has been on her mind in both positive and negative ways. She is unsure as yet on how to resolve this situation. In the meantime she received a call from a close friend with whom she used to party until the midnight hour and later. Now settled, she asked Janice to consider joining a health club with her, or signing up to take a class together.

50

BRUCE IS A CREATIVE person who has self-published one book and is now preparing to begin another. At his workplace a pleasant atmosphere should prevail, providing both he and nearby coworkers can avoid making sharp or cutting comments. Robin, the older woman at the next terminal, often will get into cutting conversations with him. She just celebrated her 60th birthday, and she really didn't want to be reminded of it. She is quite aware of his interest in Janice and his hopes that she will love him too. Is there a bit of jealousy in the air? Bruce can't really picture that, because Robin already has a man who she thinks is the one who really loves her. Then why would she be so upset about Bruce liking Janice? This is quite a mystery to him, and with mental energy being high, a debate or serious discussion would benefit from today's patterns. Both Bruce and Janice have tried to convince Robin to give up her tobacco habit, which she doesn't seem to want to do.

Bruce felt that his ability to go into details without losing perspective would be further enhanced by Janice's presence. He thanked her to himself even if not outright. He also felt as though it would take a very skilled person to trip him up because his thinking and wit should be quick and brilliant—exactly what he has observed in Janice. The combination of the two of them in tandem he felt could take them to the Promised Land.

Security and stability were important, especially to Janice as a single parent of three girls. It's not unusual for one in Janice's position to put security and stability above everything else, including thoughts of romance and other personal escapades. Yet it was the appearance of having a well-balanced life which launched him into orbit and cast his feelings fluttering. But it wasn't only because of her, rather the feelings of his own security being in flux that made Bruce prefer to stay in rather than go out, whether on weeknights or weekends.

Coming to a decision regarding the matter of his feelings toward Janice was a different ballgame. He now made no secret that he would like to get to know her on a more personal level, and honestly felt that with time it should be easier as pressure and obstacles that have been blocking the way are likely to clear up. At least that was what he was counting on, and that he would be proud to reveal his attraction for her.

51

UNLIKE BRUCE, JANICE WOULD be the beneficiary of a supportive network. The stars are now working in her favor. For a while relationships have been a little tense at home with Krystal and Jamicia battling each other and the new concerns regarding her father's health—in addition to the see-saw feelings involving Bruce. She now senses that he has loving feelings for her, and as distracting as this can be, a part of her feels that she can love him as well. She would consult a close friend whom she feels could provide advice and a calming influence that would allow her to see all these problems in a different light.

The friend was also ready to spill the beans on her own life. She would tell Janice that for once in her life she feels she has found a suitable romantic companion, but because she is a busy professional woman who has been working long and often irregular hours they have had trouble really getting together for more than the occasional chat.

Janice suggested to her that she may want to arrange a romantic lunch if his schedule will also allow for it, then strongly suggested they plan ahead for some fun things when warmer weather arrives, such as a trip to an amusement park. This, she told her, can help restore harmony if she and her perspective partner are having problems. She should do what she could to show him that she cares just for him if indeed that is the case.

Wishing and hoping for improvements in her own life, Janice would go over an invitation she recently received. She felt that attending this special event would be uplifting and entertaining. She would dress well as displaying her personal charm could help increase her popularity. A single lady seeking companionship could benefit from this romantic interval. But deep down inside she feels that any man she could fall for would feed her a bunch of lies to break her heart just as both of the fathers of her girls had done so long ago.

52

JANICE WOULD TRY HER best to take in the constructive criticism she received from her friend. Like receiving a loving boost from some goddess, the atmosphere is quiet throughout the morning hours, so there wouldn't be too much happening to slow her down. For now she would feel good about herself and what life has to offer. At a special luncheon today honoring a departing coworker she would sit next to Bruce for a time, and they would actually have a pleasant few words. He casually mentioned to her that he was stood up for a date a couple of weeks back and hasn't really ventured out much since.

Bruce's creative juices were flowing, allowing for increased competency and productivity. At work he would do his best to strive further, not having as yet any idea that contrary to conventional wisdom this would be a form of gambling with his future. Robin, for one, would assume that he is after bigger and better things and could squeeze her out.

Romance now casts a special glow as Bruce envisions being out with Janice during the nighttime, causing him to be restless and nearly sleepless most of the time. Although not going as far as expecting a committed union, he envisioned the two of them being able to share a happy rapport, although conflicting trends may put a damper on planned activities. He felt in his mind that they could work it out should any issues arise in regards to her position as his lead person interfering with a potential relationship. All they would need to do is to use discretion and not share unnecessary information concerning their off-campus activities. He hoped there would be no "things I should have said" syndrome later on. He also had in mind to defy the conventional wisdom that having a relationship with a coworker can bring about distraction. He now felt that Janice was all he would need to inspire him to be the best worker he could be and create a foundation for success.

He also contemplated buying a special item just for her. Although at times considered cheap by some who had crossed his path before, he was not one to purchase second best if shopping for a special item. If he doesn't have enough money to cover the cost of better quality, he would wait until he did.

For now, though, he would let the four winds blow and see where they would take him, in the hope that he could be happy together with Janice.

53

WHEN A MAN LOVES a woman, even if it's only a perception, it can create an uneasy feeling if that love is not reciprocated. As the time unfolds Bruce would experience a sense of unease, complicated by dread of what the reaction by Janice would be when he finally gets the nerve to come clean regarding his attraction toward her. It is this very dread that causes him to waiver on the issue. It would affect his life at home much more demonstrably than on the job. At this time the advantage for him was that he didn't have anyone really to answer to. He would leave tedious chores such as cleaning for another day, and would delegate such to other people if he had the authority. As his sole responsibility off duty he delegated to the person he hoped he'd become. At work was where he felt he was in good hands as long as he did what needed to be done in a timely manner, always being ready to do what needed to be done and then some.

Robin was one both Bruce and Janice felt talked too much. But this would be a far cry from what was now being talked about behind the scenes, where a plot to thwart Bruce's attempt to get closer to Janice was currently being orchestrated by a male worker who once was a boss but got demoted, who also has some interest in Janice. He currently has one main female accomplice in this but is looking to recruit a few more. He could even resort to bribery in order to get the mission accomplished.

That's how it is right now, but at this point Bruce is totally unaware of anything.

In his off duty hours, Bruce would strive to avoid anything that could increase discomfort. A pre-existing health condition could very well be aggravated due to the emotional upset caused by his liking for Janice and corresponding fear related to it. Even though he is not suffering from any current ailment, he would feel under the weather due to doing and especially thinking too much. It was getting hard to bear.

On this evening Laura called and wondered why Bruce hasn't called her recently. He explained that he has been busy at work and tired, something she can relate to easily as her job gets to her all the time. She knows nothing about his obsession with Janice and has no reason to tell her. But if he is forcibly separated from her he feels as if he will go crazy.

That does not mean that he doesn't have something critical to say, because he does. But it would be wiser to talk with a neighbor or family member. Since he really has neither, his best substitute is a man he sometimes orders his favorite candy from. And he tried to tell him to tread very carefully because while a company can't really take action based on feelings they certainly can, based on certain actions.

While Bruce was hoping for some soul deep moments with her, Janice was busy preparing for a party at which her cooking skills would earn her plenty of kudos from guests and the family when she prepared a special meal.

54

THE GATHERING WAS A positive moment for Janice. She would now expect each day to be a good day when she could make steady progress in all sectors of her life. She would begin this day on a healthy note with a nutritional breakfast and a workout at the local gym or on her own. A neighbor of hers has for a long time tried to convince her to move towards a healthier lifestyle but keeps putting it off. It now appears as if she may be ready to take this step. For sure she has used a lot of new muscles and is often sore afterwards. She has wanted to lose weight, and finally chose to take some steps to change her diet and lifestyle based on the latest research. She would avoid going on a fad diet, however, as she had been told that they often don't work very well.

Although there had been a lull in the workload at her job, this is all about to change shortly, as some new business would soon be upon her department, undoubtedly putting to an end the fairly easy days and leaves her breathless by day's end.

In a discussion with her neighbor, Jackie, she was told that she might try to combat the additional stress by taking an interest in alternative healing methods, yoga, or meditation—that these all could be of great benefit if she needed to learn to slow down and calm her mind. As she will soon be transferring to a newly created department at work, she knows that energetic action could lead to successfully completing all of each day's tasks. She might even receive more than a mere thank you in appreciation of a job well done.

In the back of her mind, however, is what Bruce's reaction will be once this happens. Will he think she is running away from him? Will he become bolder knowing that she will no longer be his lead person? There will be much to be sorted out, including the state of her feelings which are both pro and con. There are little things he does she can find appealing, and yet the whole dynamic involved in the thought of a workplace romance that are cause for skepticism.

55

JANICE NOW FOUND HERSELF in relaxing mode. This would be an excellent day to discard a long-time personal habit that is no longer needed or useful, or to make positive and refreshing changes to her daily routine. Without splurging too much, which she couldn't afford to do, she set about updating her wardrobe. This action was inspired after friends and coworkers commented on how they thought her current choices were old-fashioned. Nothing like being pulled over by the fashion police!

Although no longer a young girl, she felt that adjusting or improving her fitness regime could provide a head start to getting into desired trim or fitness by summertime. She is a well-proportioned woman as is, but once she really gets in shape she could indeed catch the eye of one whom she hopes could give her some loving. A black mark on an otherwise tranquil day would occur when she hears a song on the radio which brought back some painful memories of a love affair which went south when she learned of some of his dealings.

Janice is also ready to move forward in personal affairs today, freeing up delays with paperwork, communication, and contracts. Especially freeing would be putting the finishing touches on the agreements to partner with her friend Brenda in the beauty supply business. She needed to think long and hard about this one as she already had a draining full-time job in addition to being the single parent of three girls. But Brenda understood, telling her that she could do just as much or as little as she can handle until she is ready to take on more.

With Bruce still in the background, her house of love and romance has some confusion in it. But she wouldn't miss the chance to spend time with a special companion. She has one male friend she spends time with on occasion, although not intimately. And today they would spend quality time to visit the sites, meander around an art gallery, and then head off to the movies for a relaxing afternoon, needing no extra persuasion.

56

BRUCE, MEANWHILE, WOULD SPEND much of the day in his room. While desiring a more diverse life than has been the case recently, mixed trends would now prevail. A major personal influence occurs when the closest person he has to being a life coach advised him that he may be dealing with a potential heartbreaker when it comes to Janice. He was able to sense erratic actions in regards to the whole scenario, and when he returns to work on Monday he should be extra careful, allowing the chips to fall where they may. Upon hearing this he knew for sure he can expect to have some difficulty focusing. He went on to advise Bruce that if he is trying his best to solidify a new friendship or a romantic relationship, it may be wise to pull back for a week or so because effort applied now could be futile. Yet the turn of the current dynamic of his life seemed to marry Venus, the goddess of love and money, with his work life, as she waved her magic over his house of work.

For Janice, her ability to pull people together on the job and to attract needed resources was increasing. Under these forces she could receive extra perks that would serve to make employment conditions that much more agreeable for her.

Living in a bad part of town, however, would be a prominent negative dynamic to her life. And although she considers having to deal with the pathologies kind of a drag, due to her family and especially her grandmother who for the most part raised her, she retains strong ties to the area even though she would like to allow the girls a better education and environment.

On this rainy night Bruce and Janice would have different issues working for them. He is home alone contemplating his next move to bring her closer, while she is trying to determine how to tell him in a tactful way that if they were to begin a relationship that it could feel as though part of her life was being taken from her.

57

NOW COULD BE AN opportune time for one or the other to make an implied move in the other's direction at least. Despite some of her misgivings and forlorn attitude toward the idea she still feels some attraction toward Bruce. A close friend had told Janice that if she has been waiting for the opportunity to impress Bruce, now is the time. The friend reminded her that enjoying a few of life's luxuries can be the incentive needed to work harder to obtain desired goals, including men. And that such positive action and practical plans can move forward if energy is applied correctly. With all this in mind her friend would accompany Janice to the mall to help her select an appealing outfit which was about as sexy as she could get away with wearing in the workplace. "When Bruce sees you in this," the friend told her, "he is likely to imagine that you are ripe and ready for some good lovin'." And Janice snapped it up, but was not sure as to when she would wear it.

On the work front a creative approach would help resolve problems and perhaps open up some doors of opportunity. When he would spot a problem Bruce would consult Paula, the department supervisor, so that she could direct things to the proper places within the facility. Of course he usually went through Janice first if she were around. He of course hoped that being near Janice would empower him straight to the Promised Land. However, some of his more brilliant ideas might not make the grade just yet, so it may be prudent to put these on hold for a week or two before proposing them in public. He would not go right to Janice where work suggestions were concerned, because he knew she was not high up enough in the company to authorize change. But what he would go to her with would be his confession of the feeling he has for her, if only to get it off his chest. But he now needs to wait for the right time, whenever that may be.

The things people do for love can be astonishing. For Bruce it would be going out of his way as much as he can to keep her sunny side in focus. He dreams of one day the two of them being in a committed union and likely to share happy rapport and companionship. Still completely unaware of the sinister forces working against him, he would opt for an early night, dreaming that he and Janice could strengthen loving ties even further. By now he sometimes cried in his sleep over this. His attraction toward her was now as solid as a rock.

58

UNABLE TO ACHIEVE SUBSTANTIAL sleep, Bruce would phone the psychic hotline he sometimes uses. When he asked about his dilemma, the reader told him that starred times were ahead, that favorable planetary trends would now prevail, and that home life was highlighted from now until March 14. He would be sure to mark that date on the calendar, automatically figuring that this date was destined to have some special aura to it. What he hoped was that Janice would by then have a significant role in his life. At this point he wished to be able to tell her that anything she would want or need, she's got it. And he is somebody who split with a couple of women who wanted too much. And then along came crazy Mary, who wanted to hamstring him so much, automatically assuming that she could wave a magic wand and do what she wanted. Bossy women have never been his thing. But for some reason he feels he could take more from this one.

Active patterns now fire up his sector of workplace conditions, and Janice would now assume the role of jokes, along with others within the department. Joining workers named Susan, Julie, and Nettie in teasing him and trying to ascertain whom he might have a crush on, he grew red with embarrassment. He was currently the lone male member of the department on this shift.

Once she left the workplace, Janice had other things on her mind. When telling one of her friends that she may consider a move, she was told that it would be advisable to put extra physical energy into adding value and freshness to her home by decorating, painting, or remodeling, and to lessen the chance of conflict, not to insist on a certain color scheme. The urge for new home ownership now becomes stronger and this would be a good time for her to begin the process. The values appreciation going on not far away may be coming her way, increasing the chance of a good return.

Janice's friend, whose name is Donna, also advised her that when applying for a mortgage, stay cool if making a good impression with the bank is a priority. And it no doubt is, when considering that she is employed in that industry.

59

BRUCE NOW HOPED FOR conditions to be favorable for Janice to become his party doll. After all, it was her confession a few weeks back that she had been quite a party girl that became a focal point of his attraction for her. But he does have some misgivings when it comes to actually making the confession. And while it's not unusual for one to attract and eventually even marry someone that you work with, it now seems to be looked down upon more. He dreams about going out to party with her, but the alarm clock wakes him and shakes him often before it's over. Because his emotions have become so fragile, he now needs to take extra care if handling sharp or hot instruments. Before leaving home he would double check to be sure appliances are turned off. On this morning he heard something chirp like a bird, and knew what to do—that this meant it was time to replace batteries in fire detection units. He would get all this done before heading in to his workplace.

Although Janice wouldn't really admit it, she felt some attraction toward Bruce as well. Without mentioning anyone by name she did make an informal comment to a coworker that she would like to meet one with whom even the bad times could be good. She told Janice that if she is looking for romance over the next few days, it is time to get physical, to obtain the look that would get one's head to turn. She suggested that she go and head off to the nearest gym or health club, and that even if she doesn't happen to meet the perfect partner, her body will thank her for the exercise.

It was also another day on which she would try to detour Bruce's thoughts away from her. She and a couple of others would begin by hinting that local travel may provide a chance for singles such as him to mingle with potential romantic interests. There is probably some such happening close by, so he should go out of his way to put himself in a favorable spot, because you never know who you might meet.

Janice was in for an unpleasant surprise when she arrived home. Her two oldest girls were bickering with each other to the point where she was really ashamed of them. But she would need to do the proverbial count to ten before speaking. Because someone at home could be a little agitated and hard to get along with, she would need to guard against her own impatience and impulsive actions that may lead to disharmony. And by bedtime she would use all the diplomacy she could muster in order to rescue the girls from a disruptive dispute.

60

AFTER QUELLING A VOLATILE dispute involving the girls the night before, powerful energies remain. It was like she was on a carousel going round and round and up and down. When it comes to love and money, themes of obsession or possessiveness are likely to pervade the atmosphere. There was a man in another office who exhibited such jealousy over Bruce's attention toward Janice that before long both of them would have nowhere to run. In sensing that Janice may have Bruce shaking all over, regardless of if it is really so or not, intensity now rises, and this man sensed that exaggerated feelings need to be curbed to prevent an overly smothering or jealous behavior toward each other. George Singletary, the man who's most involved, told her that he needed her to come by him. It was at this time that he asked Janice point blank whether Bruce has made any overtures toward her. She said not really, but got the hint that he has his finger on the pulse of something not welcome.

Competition on the job could be fierce, even though the department is experiencing some increase in workload. After conferring with George and also his co-conspirator Gloria Sampson, Janice now sensed the possibility that someone may engage in underhanded actions to further their own career. As much as George would rave on about Bruce being too indiscreet, it is known that he has his own reputation as a ladies' man and may even consider him an obstacle in his own pursuit of Janice.

For now Bruce still doesn't sense anything out of the ordinary. He would spend the evening hours in his room contemplating his next move when it comes to Janice. During the workday Robin had asked him if he liked to travel. He said that it hasn't happened lately, but the last time he went traveling for pleasure he encountered unexpected delays, disruptions, and problems with finances. The latter situation has been a hindrance to his being able to travel as he hasn't had much work.

Having nobody really special in his life right now, Laura, his sometimes companion notwithstanding, Bruce now felt as if words of devotion spoken by someone very special could be especially meaningful. And he now hoped that someone could possibly be Janice.

61

FOLLOWING THE MEETING JANICE had with George, it would serve to be the beginning of a changeable time in her relationship with Bruce. With both travel and romantic vibes higher this morning, Bruce would do some day tripping, going off on a day-long joyride—something he used to do with much more regularity. Today would offer the perfect chance for him to meditate on how best to let the other half of his hoped for union know of his interest and devise a plan of action for doing so. He automatically assumed that she was unattached at the moment, as by this time he was sure he would have known were this not the case. He now felt as if he needed her more than ever.

Yet she was working behind the scenes on other things. One of her priorities was arranging a vacation to an exotic destination which could reveal more than interesting sites and scenery. She now would check her calendar and see where she could possibly work it in between work and the needs of her girls.

At the same time a group of friends who have been meeting regularly for a special purpose over a long period of time might now decide that it is time to disband and move on. And although this decision is bound to have an element of sadness, it could also contain a sense of renewal and relief as more time becomes available for other personal aims. When other responsibilities get in the way there is futility in any attempt to run away from it.

Bruce also was able to recall when a social group he was quite active in busted for the very reason that its core members got married or otherwise moved on to other things. But for now his chief interest is trying to win Janice's affections. She lives on the poor side of town with its share of pathologies. But this is of little concern, as he has been into similar neighborhoods before. But they would need to seek out entertainment in other areas because there isn't much available in her area.

62

AS A RESULT OF his fixation for Janice, Bruce would find the present time frame to be a mixed bag. He would try and do his best to take it easy and enjoy himself. As a self-published writer he might be eager to finish a project. However, he would then need to be prepared for an argument with one who might wish to urge him to go to a party and socialize. Laura, the one main woman in his life currently, is surely not a party person. But there is another woman who calls on him now and then who now wishes for him to go somewhere. She is one he feels imposes on him in unreasonable ways. She did have a so-called sugar daddy in her life at one time, and maybe she is just lonesome since he's been gone. He considers her a great kisser, but she is also a user, and is always asking for cigarettes and money. He knows that she is unlikely to be impressed by his attempt to juggle work and home life. But eventually he does give in, at least this time.

Since he was invited to a relaxing party and social gathering, he would take the opportunity to unwind and relax. But it would not contribute to his happiness the way he now felt Janice could, and counted on one day being able to set bells off inside her. At the same time the loss of sleep and the worry over her sapped his energy. Therefore he knew that heavy, labor-intensive chores should be postponed until his vim and vitality are at a peak, which isn't today.

He for sure doesn't want to involve his workmates in his current mood toward Janice, and so he will discuss the issue with one he has known well over a few years. He would need to be prepared for criticism from any close or not-so-close friend but would no doubt refuse in any way to acknowledge or accept advice unless it is both constructive and practical. For sure he would not get the good vibrations from any discussion of this issue.

So Bruce would phone a woman he knew from a former job, knowing that she would be able to give him a detached viewpoint. She tried to give a few pointers, but couldn't take much time as she had some important tasks to get to. Having a one-track mind made him resentful of her shortness with him on the phone. He could be both grateful and resentful of one who could tell it like it is. Once he did his pause to count to ten, he would then be able to keep in mind that sometimes other people have their own agenda.

63

ARMED WITH THE HOPE that one fine day Janice would be his girl, Bruce would be propelled into sensitive mode. This is apt to be an emotional time as agitation and upsets could create some deep-seated problems while his mindset concerning Janice comes to the full in regal love-splendor dreams. The domineering and demanding antics of certain associates could test his tolerance and resolve. This could be especially true of Robin. He has been blown away by some of her acerbic comments.

He hopes that his fondness for Janice won't be just a dream. It has led to him tossing and turning for several nights, unable to get to sleep for the longest time. She has gotten him to the point to where lightning was striking, with her being in his mind nearly all the time. Being within a workplace meant that he would need to restrain his impatience in order to reduce the risk of arguments and disharmony.

When his workday was finished he was bedeviled by loss of sleep, yet ready for some change. If he got the chance, he would do something different, new, or unusual to add pleasure and variety to his day. Fulfillment of this would come when Sue, a woman whom he contacted through this Internet dating site, called and encouraged him to meet for a meal and conversation. It took some persuasion to get him to do so, but he did. It was an okay meeting, but no further dates were planned. Their outlooks on life seemed to be vastly different.

It is often said that silence is golden, and that would be the case now. The friendly if sometimes overbearing banter of the past couple of weeks would now be a thing of the past. If anything, his ego could take a beating. The one at his workplace who wanted to be quite a lover, along with his female accomplice, were busy behind the scenes plotting their dirty work.

Bruce was now beginning to get the first hints that maybe something wasn't quite right. If he were to know that someone on the job doesn't like him, he might then need to take extra care because they for sure may try to cause problems or tell a few untruths designed to damage his reputation. There would then be no stop to their dance of betrayal.

64

SENSING THAT THE WORKPLACE scene could now be a bumpy ride, Bruce would do his best to remain cool and calm. Yet he still retained the desire to someday be able to take Janice to Loveland. This would be another day when he would find the gods not smiling as brightly as they had been. Unbeknownst to him, a woman in another office was asking some people if they have heard the latest. Upon responding in the negative, she filled them in on the perceived romance involving Bruce and Janice, along with details on the plot to get Bruce ousted, or at the very least to thwart whatever plan there was for any sort of rendezvous. Tears would be falling on Bruce's pillow once this goes through and he realizes that Janice is not his Venus and won't be.

Minor obstacles and problems are likely to hinder progress as the new account they had been expecting has now landed. However, he knows that if he is flexible and willing to make adjustments along the way, some progress can be made.

His relationship with Janice would now begin to sink like quicksand. She was not as open toward him as had been the case for some time. For now at least he is attributing this turn of events to a now increasing workload, which obviously would erase time for casual banter. He still would do what he could to give her the work any way she wants it, but now has this foreboding sense that it would not win her over on a personal level. And still her presence made him look forward to going to the job each day more than was customary in his working life. To him even the bad times could be good as long as she was around. In his mind she must sense that he has taken a fancy toward her, but has still not mustered the courage to come clean with her and yet wants to. The daunting uncertainty as to whether he should or shouldn't would reach a fever pitch to the point of causing him to break out in a cold sweat. He is not sure what he should do.

Bruce's relationship with Janice, who was first and foremost a business associate as opposed to a friend, might experience a few ups and downs, making it difficult to know exactly where he stands. It was a beautiful morning when he left for work this day, but a steady cold rain was falling as he made the drive home. This suited his now subdued mood as he fears that Janice will not run to him the way that he hoped for. He would try to keep financial talk and dealings out of the equation because that could muddy the waters even further. While having a good responsible job makes him feel as though she would never have to ask him for money as others who have crossed his path have, the fact that she is not only a work associate but his lead person muddies the waters further, but doesn't appear to be putting the brakes on his desire to be loved by her. But it is putting the brakes on as far as developing the nerve to express these thoughts to her.

Making allowances for the shortcomings of the people he resides with could also test his patience and resolve, which was now in short supply. The older man who lives in the room next to his often will ask him if the mail had arrived, and his apparent obsession with this tends to get on his nerves a bit. The two have never been close, but yet one time when in casual conversation he said that he might move elsewhere, he begged him not to, not wanting Bruce to tell him goodbye.

65

WITH HIS SENSE THAT troublesome activities may be occurring at work, Bruce had the foreboding sense that the day might seem to go from bad to worse. However, if he is able to keep smiling and present a happy demeanor, he felt that he could come through unscathed. Physical energy was now apt to be low, which would also reduce motivation and enthusiasm. This is something he would not wish to happen, as he needed to always strive toward perfection.

He would continue to be inspired by his hopes and wishes, but would remain realistic in deciding how to go about bringing these to fruition. In the romance stakes, Bruce seemed to have the luckless knack and could easily be led astray by wishful thinking. There may not be people laughing at him behind the scenes, but he has often had the dubious and lonely distinction of being in the wrong place at the wrong time. And his interest in Janice now appears to be heading in that direction as well, leaving a hole of doubt.

Daydreaming is fine, but he can't allow this to get out of hand. When this happens he sometimes dreams of Janice and him lounging away on distant shores. On one recent day she called Bruce into the next room to point out some errors that were uncovered in his work. There were six of them, and at this point he felt about as tall as Tom Thumb. This may have been before his interest in her personally really took off. But it did cause him a bit of paranoia nonetheless.

He never had much success in meeting women when out in the partying scene, regardless of what he tried to open a conversation with. Once he even suggested that maybe he would score better were he bold enough to start with something such as "Hey, baby, let's screw." It was for this reason that when he learned that Janice was quite a party girl at one point and still does so occasionally, he felt that it was really saying something, that it was an area of life where he was substantially cheated.

At the same time Bruce knew that Janice had a lot of obligations as the single mother of three girls. If a challenging situation regarding a child arises, she may need to put aside daily chores and especially social life for a short period to find a satisfactory solution to the problem. This had sometimes been divisive in past situations where he had his sights set on dating a woman who had young children. But these days it is seldom an issue as in most cases the children would be grown. However, before anything like this can be discussed, he would first need to get up the nerve to tell her directly of his attraction to her.

66

WITH THE ADDITION OF the new account the firm landed, the work is steadier than it had been over the previous few weeks. In a frank discussion with one he knew, Bruce was advised to be very careful. If he felt he must come clean, he should proceed slowly and he would be glad he took his time in choosing the right direction or action. Yet he was so wound up over this that he felt that he might as well be climbing a mountain. At times his mind would wander as minor restlessness consumes his thoughts. He would surely need to be wary of impulsive behavior that could cause a mishap. By now Bruce was convinced that he loved Janice and wanted her to be his girl.

Robin would remind Bruce that if he hasn't yet made restaurant reservations, bought a card, and/or arranged the perfect gift for Valentine's Day, it is time to get moving. Her boyfriend from a distance is coming up to see her for the holiday.

Bruce found it to be kind of a drag that progress was now moving more slowly than he once felt it had. He had hoped by now that one weekend night he would be in Janice's company and that they would go somewhere to drink, dance, and let it all hang out. He had been told by one coworker who knows her quite well that she is an entirely different person once she is away from the workplace.

At the same time work behind the scenes would progress smoothly. He was unaware of this, but others in the facility were told that Bruce is here now, but if they have their way he will soon be gone. Keeping quiet about this special project or venture would be a good move, as they would wait to reveal what they are doing until options become a little clearer. Well aware of the litigious world they're living in, they would need to do what they could not to yak too much, or else they could be hit with a lawsuit should he choose to pursue.

Janice would spend this evening visiting a sick colleague who is now confined at home after being released from the hospital. She was told that she is fortunate to still be alive. She now hopes to make a full and complete recovery, but won't be back to work for a few more weeks. For her part Janice was glad that she was able to bring her some cheer.

67

AFTER SEEMINGLY BEING ON needles and pins for weeks, Bruce would now find things to be more on the quiet side, at least for a while. The work atmosphere is fairly silent today, which should satisfy his current mood. Above all he is trying to convince himself that it's all right, and that in due time the chance to tell Janice of his attraction will manifest itself and everything will be fine. The increasing work volume would lend a more solemn atmosphere, and if one needed to see Janice about any issue she would need to tell them to hold on until she can get there.

If he was seeking absolute peace and quiet, he would need to make a special effort to go off somewhere tranquil to be alone. And that's what he would do following the workday. His eyes were not focused on Janice as much as usual, as he now assumes the time will come when he can be with her, and was sure that it would be his moment in rapture.

Being peaceful has not been easy for Bruce in recent times. He has been haunted by the notion that the day of reckoning may soon come, at which time he will be forced to walk like a man and face the music. As an effort to keep his mind off negativities and in attempt to find a pearl in the oyster of life, he could be drawn to assisting other people in a practical manner or to performing some type of charity work. An acquaintance told him that were he to act on these compassionate urges, emotional gratification can very well be his reward. But his thoughts soon would wander back to Janice, as in his mind he is trying to pinpoint what it is about her that has driven him to the point he finds himself now. He reasoned that it is just some of her ways that formed the basis of his attraction. And yet she also has other ways he finds very unattractive, and wishes to do everything in his power to keep that side of her at bay. He now hopes never to lose that certain feeling for her.

Opting for a quiet evening, he would contemplate getting a therapeutic massage, but vetoes the idea due to cost considerations. He then tries going shopping alone but ends up not buying anything more than a sandwich. He then figures that time spent in a library on the Internet researching a topic of interest could appeal as he didn't have a busy schedule.

After his stint at the library an evening at home would be the perfect conclusion to the working week. He would fix himself a meal of meatloaf and mashed potatoes, then retire shortly after, ready to dream a little dream of Janice.

68

THE WEEKEND WOULD BE variable for both concerned parties. This morning Bruce was apt to again prefer a quiet time or even a period of solitude where he can be alone with his thoughts. He now knows that in a few days Janice will be in a new department at work and would not be in her presence much, and it is causing him to go to pieces. Later in the day he would go to a psychic reader a few miles from home. This gypsy woman told him that he should not have any ill effects from this situation and that no doubt Janice has some attraction for him as well. She added, however, that facing up to problems rather than trying to run away or duck for cover would be advised.

Following the reading he would spend some time partaking in one of his other interests, that being trying to convince retailers to carry his favorite candy, one that used to be nearly everywhere but which now is rather hard to come by, and wishes he had more success with it.

However, following his mid-morning excursion to the psychic, he lost his desire for going into action. As a rule he is normally always ready to fight or help resolve a crisis, and taking this type of action now could lead to the most productive results. But for now he was in the mood to let the world pass him by. He would wait until another day to do all this.

At the same time Janice has a special date this evening with someone she had met at a bus stop the previous weekend when heading downtown. He may not turn out to be the love of her life, but nevertheless thought that this was a perfect time to update her image with a new hairstyle or outfit that will make just the impression she is hoping to create.

For Bruce yesterday's subdued mood continued into this day and evening. While Janice was out and about, he would while away the time at home, bogged down by the cue that he may not get the chance to ever party with her.

69

BY NOW BRUCE HAD sensed that the outlook for him being able to have any kind of affair with Janice was only fair at best. Yet his physical stamina is regenerated, making this a good time to begin whatever has personal appeal or importance. He might still not have a lot of enthusiasm for household chores or tasks requested by other people.

He would go to a shopping mall and take a stroll just to get out of the house for a spell. While there he encountered a surprise when someone out of his past spotted him and beamed, "Hello, stranger." It was Barbara Dobson, a woman he dated some fifteen years back. She was quite a wild thing back in the day, and as they recounted a few of their escapades, her reply was that everybody needs somebody to love at times. She talked as though she would still be ready, willing and able to do their thing if he was in the mood to reconnect. Her mood was animated, but all that occurred this day was that she gave him her number should he wish to connect.

And while this was a welcome diversion from current affairs his mind would once again be weakened by worry as soon as he arrived back at home. He would return to the workplace on the following day, but now with somewhat less vigor. He sensed that someone may be deceiving him or hiding something, and that it would be better if he knew or were told about it. As he spent time trying to contemplate what his next move should be, he recalled that a member of a club he once belonged to had an innate talent for snooping and getting to the bottom of things. He would attempt to contact this person as he might need to utilize this talent now.

Creative urges were now strong, and these could possibly be an antidote to what has become one of his loneliest periods in several years. Only an encounter with Janice would remove this feeling totally, but sticking to a planned format could prove frustrating due to an acute lack of patience. So he'd wait until tomorrow and try again.

70

WISHING HE COULD BEGIN the rest of his days with Lady Janice and Lord Bruce showering each other with fortunate vibes, he wanted to convince himself that he wouldn't need to rely on any kind of good luck charm in order to receive rewards. Janice seemed a little more vibrant again today, as he overheard her talking to some coworkers about that being the way men are. He didn't interject into the conversation, but to himself he sensed that the comment was more in jest as opposed to any kind of sarcasm. His appreciation of her humor was a key component to his desire to have someone like her as part of his life.

Opportunities for him to increase his bank account were foreseen as he could work long enough to erase the doldrums of the past year. With the increased workload overtime could become available and could afford him the opportunity for him to be able to take Janice someplace where they could dance. This is his dream, even if he has to travel through some of the city's mean streets as a consequence.

Going dancing with Janice is his main goal at this time. It wouldn't matter if no sexual liaison developed. And this was an incentive for him to continue his good work and to continue showing ambition. By doing so he figured that it could soon lead to a pay raise or a promotion which could make it easier for him to budget more successfully, all the while looking ahead toward working his way to having a place in Janice's life.

When he looked her way he would feel funny inside, really desiring to get to know her better away from the prying eyes of the workplace.

Furthermore, he would take the time on his way home to buy a lottery ticket and also enter a sweepstakes contest in hope that it could increase the chance of a lucky streak. He would still feel incomplete as long as Janice still didn't occupy an entry on his calendar of events. His top priority was to be able to get with her and have some fun one night. And suddenly buoyed with optimism, he would now hope for fruition.

Janice was now spending a much smaller portion of the workday at her desk located nearly across from Bruce. She is training for her new responsibility in a newly created department. She may be asked to present a lecture or to speak up at a meeting. In addition she also assumed a responsibility of helping to organize a picnic for friends and family this upcoming summer. As the daylight hours are now lengthening, she would take a ride after work to help with the sorting out of life processes.

This evening she would spend some time brushing up on her proposed presentation and make the revisions which she felt would end up with her words more likely to be received positively by the audience. Following this, home should be a fun place this evening, especially as friends and family members would drop by for a visit. She would play a wish upon a star game with her girls plus a couple of friends' children. It would be a satisfying and enjoyable experience for those participating.

Bruce would sense some optimism at the moment. But if he began thinking that his get it done attitude regarding the workload would serve to bring Janice to a higher point in his life, he would soon be forced to think again.

71

BRUCE CONTINUED TO FIND it exciting being in Janice's company, and now figured her less-lively phase to be merely connected to the increased workload since the addition of the new account. Last night he meditated on the possibility of him coming clean on his attraction for her. So he phoned a psychic reader who advised him to wait a while longer, that if he spoke too soon the desired results may not be achieved.

Energy levels would be on the rise as a buzz of excitement pervades today's atmosphere. Janice seemed to be her livelier and more chatty self. Bruce would tread cautiously as far as engaging in the conversations. As his senses awakened so did his sweet spot for her, which would prove extremely hard to resist. Now the birds and bees were heavy on his mind, with his perceived buttercup just across the aisle from where he was sitting.

At the start of the New Year, Janice made an informal resolution to get in better shape. As physical fitness became an ongoing issue for her, she would try to persuade a few of her friends and coworkers to go on a regular walk or run around the park or a local shopping mall, as this can increase the chance of remaining fit and healthier well into old age.

In her more gregarious phase Janice and a few others would tease Bruce a bit in an attempt to diffuse whatever interest in her he is perceived to have. Robin in particular would chime in to this, saying things such as "listen carefully and you may hear the peal of wedding bells." On the surface at least it still appeared as though these people were friendly toward him, and as one of their single friends possibly looking for the perfect romantic match, they would now put their matchmaking skills to the test on the hunch that they could make two people very happy. Janice mentioned a couple of ladies on site who may be looking.

72

AN EXPRESSIVE MOOD WOULD now overtake Bruce. When Donna, one of the women who worked in another area from him asked him how he was today, he told her right out that he was feeling as though he could conquer the world. He added that today's main challenge is to remain positive and enthusiastic rather than succumbing to gloomy or pessimistic thoughts. And while she thought his attitude to be right on, she had no idea as to what was on his mind that moment. For him love was in the air. And while he has always appreciated feminine charm and beauty, he was now sure that there's no other like Janice. As one who has been romantically eyeing a coworker for a few weeks, he now had convinced himself that this was the time when he could be in luck. And he wouldn't turn down an offer from a staff member who wished to arrange a date with one of their colleagues. The hint that Janice was who he had his sights on had been evident for some time now.

The idea of bringing it out in the open, possible baggage notwithstanding, would now prove to be irresistible, as was the idea of the others in his department wanting to drag the truth out of him. But at this point he would remain mum, as he would seek out Janice at a time when none of them were in earshot. At this point he still felt as if there was sufficient enough attraction on her part and that the opportunity could prove very beneficial.

The time finally came at the end of the work day. He made an excuse to wait around for a few minutes after the rest of the crew had left for the day. The fact that one who was said to be a reputed playboy was plotting against him was not a hindrance, and Bruce was unaware as yet that this was occurring. He told Janice that he wanted to see her for a minute prior to leaving. He then reminded her of when she suspected that he had an interest in somebody, and then told her that it was her. Janice's response was, "Can't happen."

With that Bruce promptly left the premises for the day, satisfied that he had the audacity to come clean. If nothing else he felt it would clear the air. His soul moved into a dreamy position and thoughts of leisure, treasure, and pleasure. Accentuating love and creative pursuits would be enhanced. In free time he urged himself to express artistic talents whenever he could. Little did he know of the cruel twist of fate that would result from his confession, and that an ensuing tragedy would wrap around his psyche over the upcoming few weeks, and the tension that would permeate at his job.

73

WITH JANICE'S "CAN'T HAPPEN" remark, Bruce's dream of being able to fly out with Janice was pretty well dashed. It also provided fuel for the efforts of those who wanted to get him out, and now some would rave on, even going as far as to consider the attraction confession as sexual harassment even though no effort at obtaining favors, sexual or otherwise, were ever discussed. In Bruce's mind his dream of going to Loveland with Janice still wasn't completely dead, and he hung onto some hope that this was just a temporary setback—that she would warm to him again in due time. As the working relationship began to crash, he wondered when he would be loved by her. At the very least he wished for a return to the more cordial work environment that existed before coming clean. To him life would be a dream if he could only get that far. Of course he longed for more but did resign himself to the fact that he was not likely to be able to achieve this goal. But he wanted to at least get something out of this.

The post-confession environment may have contained the same cast of characters, but in Bruce's mind it was so radically different that he might as well have gone to the moon. Things were a lot busier than they had been for the past few weeks, with several bugs in handling the work connected with the new account, and it tended to hold up progress quite a bit. Over the next few days Bruce would need to prepare to be on the move. There would not be the time for idle chatter, and the days of occasionally going home early were now gone as well. Janice also was able to take advantage of that on several occasions; now she would often be in the office long after her crew had departed. Where Bruce was concerned, she no longer would converse with him about things not related to the job at hand. And such an about face would gnaw at his soul, and he would love to have said to her "Don't you care. You were so civil and vibrant towards me before and now you don't seem to give a damn."

Now feeling as though she was stepping on him, Bruce nevertheless tried to go the extra mile to get as much done as he could. And in a couple of weeks she would no longer be his lead, something which made him sad. Yet it could be a chance for redemption as the specter of a superior-subordinate relationship would no longer be an issue. But behind the scenes George and Gloria were working up their own brand of witchcraft, and Bruce was their target. They would recruit others to the idea that they would get him out of the place no matter what it took.

Janice would then call Bruce out into the lobby area where she told him that he needed to nip his feeling toward her in the bud. Word got to her that he wanted a transfer into her new department. He filled the application out, but scratched the idea because the schedule he had to work then would be hard to get used to. He felt as low as if he had been stood up by a beauty queen.

Throughout the day Bruce would experience problems maintaining steady focus and concentration. Instead of climbing a stairway to heaven he might have been crawling into a dark dungeon. He would just need to be careful not to take on too much or scatter his energy, which would limit his ability to complete work. Performing one task at a time, from beginning to end, should ensure that work is completed satisfactorily and deadlines are met. This is a very deadline-focused operation, and is the one thing about this job that bothers him. The type of work was in his area of expertise, yet it drove him nuts that Janice kept switching him from operation to operation. But eventually he adjusted to it, and for sure didn't want her to have to babysit him. And when his attraction for her began to take off, this set him free and kept him hanging on, even at times when he thought he might be better off elsewhere. Another agency did send a job lead his way, and he turned it down.

This whole affair did inspire some of Bruce's writing, which was his main interest away from work. He would go online to see where he might find a suitable location for a reading. Sure enough he happened to find one. Acknowledgment would be positive when he was invited to present some of his writing to an audience this evening. This pleased him but he was still not able to quit thinking about Janice.

74

EVERYBODY NEEDS SOMEBODY, IT is so often said and Bruce still felt as if Janice was the one he needed. But he would need to be very wary now that she is looking at him in a much less positive light. An incident would touch a sore point with her this morning when he told her that he wanted to make sure enough got done so she could keep her sunny side up. It was then that she said she would not go there. Nothing was meant by this other than being able to keep her in good spirits so that the more brutal side of her personality would not surface. For now, however, he had no thought of switching jobs as he would need to try to avoid carrying old emotions and battle scars into a new work situation or even a personal relationship.

He got along well with Paula, the official supervisor of the department. Now made aware of some of the efforts to get Bruce out, it would nearly cause her to go crazy. She sincerely felt that he was one of the best workers she had in the department.

With harmony quite obviously strained with a woman on the job Bruce would strive to do his best to walk tall, certain that if he continues to do the best he could at his work that he could rise above it all. But more tolerance and respect on his part may be needed to avoid further tension. This was not a good time for even the most persuasive side of him to try to push issues or force opinions. Even though he would eventually run with the football in an attempt to get other people in the department to agree with what he would say, making him think they were on his side would prove elusive. But when decision time comes they would most likely back away from any promises or commitments, instead they would say things bad about him whether or not they were pressured to do so.

Janice would find her social life away from work to be hectic. She would have an occasion to be entertaining at home. She would opt for a simple menu to reduce stress. Heaven knows this whole affair at work has created plenty of it.

75

RUMORS WERE NOW CIRCULATING at work that Bruce was a must to avoid. And yet some who were told this were at the same time counseled to try and treat him right. This way he could be kept in the dark regarding what was going down and not get wind of it.

It was, however, an excellent time for Janice, as her public persona increases as well as her power and leadership qualities. Her ability to orchestrate events at her workplace in a positive manner is enhanced. It is now true for her away from the job as well. Those involved in organizing a social function for this evening would find that plans fall into place just as envisioned. Janice arranged an outing at a club as a birthday celebration for one of her friends. The party lights shone brightly, and laughter and conviviality were in abundance as a good time was had by all those in attendance. Just about all who were invited had arrived by the nine o'clock start time, and few left much before closing time.

When she arrived home a message awaited her from a man she has dated on occasion. He wanted to know if she could go out with him the following evening. To her it sounded as if he wanted to take her on some sort of magic carpet ride. While the offer sounded inviting, she knew that she would need to find a way to keep the children entertained if she wanted some romantic time with someone. She was nervous about leaving the girls with a sitter two nights in a row for fear that they would feel unwanted and neglected, much as she felt toward her own parents when she was a child. She was raised mostly by her grandmother, whom she really adores to this day.

After sleeping on this overnight, she phoned him back in the morning and explained to him the circumstances and proposed an alternative—that being going for a walk during the afternoon. The sidewalks around her area were not exactly the boardwalk, but they would serve the purpose as a backdrop for conversation.

During the walk the man would tell her over and over how much he would like for her to be his steady date instead of just the occasional get-together. In time he would sense that something may be wrong. Upon making the inquiry Janice would tell him straight out that while she enjoys conversing with him, he is not one who could sweep her off her feet and leave her breathless. She then explained to him that being the single parent of three girls made it hard for her to always be able to go out on the spur of the moment, that the younger set would be the center of attraction for her as a solo parent, and devoting time and energy to their pursuits can produce both joy and pride. Krystal, her oldest, seems already to have a promising future in the theatrical arts and also has made some pottery. Deep down inside Janice may feel as if she is just not ready for love, at least not in the encompassing way that he is proposing.

Just a few days later things would turn in new directions. Daunted by the apparent backstabbing taking place at her current job, Janice would take a personal holiday during which she would use time to arrange an interview for a new job, while Krystal would audition for a theatrical role, and also sign up to speak at a public forum on current affairs. The school would request that she sign the permission slips. Considering that this could be a once in a blue moon opportunity, she had no qualms about doing so.

Longing to do something to celebrate Krystal's success, she then tried to figure out how to do so. The one thing that was certain was that whatever was to be on the agenda for entertainment tonight should bring pleasure and happiness. After making arrangement for the girls, Janice and a couple of friends would head for the subway to ride into the center of town to enjoy the scene.

76

AFTER A PLEASURABLE NIGHT on the town, positive trends continue for Janice, although recovering from last night could leave her a little lethargic, particularly during the morning hours. After laughing so much while out, her voice was cracked and hoarse. Therefore she would take it slow and by lunchtime she should be raring to go ahead with social plans that have been arranged. But a part of her was still full after doing the shuffle and other dances the night before, and she might have preferred to enjoy the comforts of home rather than going out to meet and mingle. Despite having made a pledge to attend this gathering, she chose the home option, thus notifying the organizer of this event of her decision. This would be a good time for her to contact the local handyman to make repairs around the house or check maintenance to ensure that everything is in good working order. As she hasn't tested smoke detectors recently, this was time for that small but important task.

Meanwhile, Bruce definitely would prefer the comforts of home over going out to meet and mingle. Things that have enveloped on the work scene have depleted his energy. Following his confession to Janice his former camaraderie with her obviously has crashed and she now seems reluctant to converse with him on anything not in direct correlation to the job at hand. For a few weeks she has built him up toward thinking that he could well be her buttercup. Yet about hearing what was conceived as being an affirmative on his end as well, she informed him that he would need to nip the attraction in the bud. In a lunchtime talk with a woman in his work area named Ruby, he expressed his concern that Janice was acting so weird toward him all of a sudden. She was of the opinion that she probably just had a lot on her mind due to the impending transfer to the new department which had been created and that she would head. He replied that he is sure going to miss her every day.

77

WHILE HE FELT THAT the conversation he had with Ruby was agreeable, he still felt as though while Janice once told him that she thought of him as a good worker, he now felt as if she were taking him for granted. When she asked him to go with her into the lobby where she told him to curb his attraction toward her, he ascertained that he would need to be alert for some disagreements at work each morning. Clearing up some unfinished business or discussions might be important to him, so agreeing to listen would be a positive step in finding a solution that they both could live with. Yet an obvious darkness surrounded the whole environment, as he sensed that she was not about to reach out to him in any way. Could it be possible, he pondered, that she had the desire to be his friend and possibly lover, and that he did not respond in kind until it was too late? Was she the one who felt spurned rather than he, and does she as a result want him to get out of her life?

Although coming from different areas, there was a fairly heavy rain this morning; so on this day both Bruce and Janice would leave a little earlier than usual for work to avoid rush hour or a delay caused by an accident. Both knew that the chances were very probable, and that the act of experiencing these types of problems can increase your frustration and stress.

Also, Bruce in particular but to some extent Janice as well, needed to be careful not to vent bad humor on colleagues or other people who could be in the line of fire. If she was once attracted to Bruce as well as he was to her, she now appeared to be totally without pity. She did not even respond when he would say good morning or good night. He found this to be particularly disturbing as he knew that she didn't like being treated that way herself. The rapport between them now wasn't pretty and it would just be a matter of time before some sort of breaking point would confirm the crash.

Janice would relieve some of her stress surrounding the situation in a different way, by going out to shop for clothes. She needed to keep tabs on spending, and especially when shopping with friends. She would be alert for bargains on last year's styles.

And as the spinning wheel of life continued to go around, Janice would make every attempt to feel good, and finding some good outfits at bargain prices would fill the bill, at least temporarily.

78

BRUCE DID ALL HE could to remain positive that this was to be only a temporary setback—that he and Janice could one day soon work it out. If his confession of attraction proved in any way disturbing, his goal was to be able to someday pay her back with interest, most likely with some sort of night out.

A pleasant change would now arrive today as a tranquil mood would culminate in his house of creative expression and romantic trends. Still fantasizing about Janice, he would search his archive of poems and song lyrics he had written in order to find one he could rewrite just for her in hope that one day he could present it to her.

In his mind the cosmos would send even more good news with the merging of her talkative mission with the bountiful joking of those around her. But he soon learned through sheer observation that the reason her sector of good spirits was so strong was because they were urging a member of the department to prepare for a happy event, although he could not determine what it was.

For now Bruce's desire for Janice to be his candy girl would continue to go unfulfilled. Meanwhile, Janice desired to get the girls into a safer neighborhood and better schools. As she has been busy searching for a new home to rent or buy, her search just may now bear fruit. As she is not too far away from where improvements are now beginning to creep in, the sale of her current property may be more profitable than she dared imagine. Another opportunity for a fresh start could also arrive with a romantic interest. A neighbor of hers has slowly been making inroads into her life.

Sensing that Janice has lost any loving feeling she may or may not have had for him, Bruce would turn his attention inward. As a creative project is nearly ready to begin, starting within the next two weeks should increase the possibility of success. The next morning he would be a couple of hours late to work as he has an appointment scheduled to discuss layout for his second self-published book endeavor.

79

SPLENDID THOUGHTS WENT THROUGH Bruce's mind in hopes that somewhere, someday fate would connect him with Janice. He was on a roll as another great day rises in the celestial heavens. He would be feeling great, and even though there were some doubts these wouldn't be a worry—that he would soon be Janice's soul man despite her current aloofness. But he wouldn't hesitate to let off some steam to others in his work area when Janice was not around. Prior to his confession they had as cordial a working team as could be possible under the auspice of her being his lead person. He tried as best he could to ascertain from others why she wasn't as friendly toward him as she had been. It now seemed in his mind as though she was his world and he wanted the good feeling back. The response which he got was that she had so much on her mind with the pending transfer to her new work area. One woman even told him that he shouldn't have fallen in love.

However, Bruce would not confess that he loved Janice, but to a few of his work mates this seemed obvious whether it was really so or not. At this point he considered writing her a short note or even letter telling her that should she wish for outside contact with him she could send him an email at his said address. It could be just a shotgun affair, but at least it would be something.

If he could arrange time off, this would be an appropriate day as Janice seemed more bogged down and more elusive even than usual as of late. He thought about going to Paula, the department supervisor, but then thought better of it as he needed to play catch-up with his finances. If not, he sought to at least do something to contribute to his happiness and joy at a later time.

Janice was getting ready for another venture as she was organizing a social function involving a family gathering coming up soon. She would concentrate on simple and elegant rather than fussy or over-the-top.

This was a suggestion given to her by one of her work associates, who assured her that if all the guests were sure to have an enjoyable time, she would be less stressed, and that her intuition wouldn't steer her wrong.

Bruce's attempt to feign a happy demeanor was short-lived. He was acting like a lonely blue boy over Janice, and it showed. He was now too much of an open book for his own good. But upon leaving for the day one of his work mates, sensing something was wrong, asked him about it. And when hesitant to reply, she said to him "It's Janice, isn't it?" He nodded his head in agreement.

80

WHEN BRUCE SAW JANICE the next day, he would try his best to be charitable toward her in hope that this might induce her to warm up to him again. At break a work mate told him that many times she will display a tough exterior but is softhearted in fact. This characteristic could be on display right now as she is getting ready to help another work associate navigate through some tough times. Robin, the woman who sits at the station next to him, just received some bad news concerning a health issue. She began to sob, saying that she had no money or insurance for medical care. Janice came right out and told her that a hospital or facility has to treat her if she walked through the door. When Robin said that nobody would care, Janice assured her that she did. But she did send Robin home for the day, as she didn't want her issues to become a disruption to the whole unit, as they most certainly would be if she stayed.

Bruce's mindset was that he somehow has got to get Janice into his life at a level beyond just work associate. But he now senses that she would just as soon see him hit the road. At least that is the vibe that he now seems to be receiving from her. As a result he would now need to tread carefully if there are mitigating factors that could come back to affect him in a negative manner. But he wants to love her so badly, and the strains are now quite evident. An impulsive mood arrives this evening as the man inside him sails through a telephone chat line to see who he might be able to hook up with to give him some lovin' as he waits for the one he really wants. Not finding any takers, he heads out to a lounge where he asks one woman if she wanted to dance. She agreed, much to his surprise, and they danced to quite a few songs. They did not, however, spend any further time together and no contact information was exchanged.

There was no real love felt for his dance partner that evening and he didn't really care since he was hurting so bad because of Janice, knowing he has to face her five days a week. He now swears that if she doesn't come around he will never love again. To attempt to divert his mindset he would suddenly decide to clean out the fridge, and also the pantry and closet areas of his room. He would be sure to recycle to a favorite charity if discarding clothes or odds and ends that no longer suit his style or requirements.

But Janice is his primary source of attention. Longing for her to be his, he continues to be disturbed by the trends that see an attitude as though she keeps running away.

81

IT WOULD BE A satisfactory day for Bruce, but he would need to keep his tendency to daydream about Janice under wraps. As he was running late for work, he would proceed to move at a steady clip but not rush, as this would have the tendency to lead to a wreck. A close call on this morning's commute caused him to be aware that a minor accident-prone period now exists. A car would attempt to twist into his lane and he had to move fast just to get out of the way. There's always the possibility that the guy or gal behind the wheel was drunk, but he obviously would have no way of proving it. And he didn't notice the license number anyway.

Upon arriving at the workplace he related this story, and as a result got a pretty stern lecture from one of the associates. "Don't you care about getting drunk drivers off the road? You should have obtained the license number and reported it." Bruce responded that not every driver who misjudges traffic is drunk.

"Drivers should slow down if normally used to speeding," the worker continued, "and be sure and remember to obey all rules of the road." By now Bruce replied that no harm was done, so why continue to dwell on it.

Janice was not in her usual space right away. This was the day on which she went to a job interview and also for a performance review for her soon-to-be former position. She was dressed a bit more stylishly than usual, and as a result she was likely to make a good impression, as long as she was to answer the questions asked and refrain from saying too much. In reality the interview was just a formality, as she already had the position as lead of this newly created department. However, she sensed that discussions surrounding her relationship toward Bruce were likely, and someone could offer timely assistance or advice. She, in fact, was informed that actions were being taken to oust him, but she was not to say anything.

The beat goes on as Janice would continue to act quite aloof toward Bruce, knowing he would soon be gone. Not officially involved, this conspiracy project with a solid foundation would most likely prosper, providing actions remain honest and above board. But her gut feeling tells her that things are being done deceptively.

82

IT HAD BECOME A very upsetting time for Bruce. From the time of his arrival at work until the end of the day he would feel as though he were walking a tightrope, totally bedeviled by Janice's near total tuning out. When he confessed his attraction to her, he felt he was doing the right thing, that it would clear the air and that they would continue to work together in peace and harmony. By now, it had become painfully obvious that it hadn't worked out that way. The tension was so great that you could cut it with a knife. He has literally had a case of the blues since the good feeling she once seemed to have has been gone. As he experienced some feelings of frustration and distress, he may be applying energy in such a way that achievements become way too difficult. In a psychic reading he was told that she should start warming up to him in a week or so. "That'll be the day," he said to himself. The week passed and she still hadn't removed her cool façade.

Bruce wanted to be a believer in the power of psychic phenomena. After all, the reader he spoke with enjoys a very high accuracy rating, according to the online research he did. She had something like 86 percent satisfaction. And yet that still leaves 14 percent to chance, and it now looked to him as if this was going to be one of those times.

Distress notwithstanding, he still felt that hard work combined with steady productivity could be his reward as long as he didn't take for granted those who were trying to assist his efforts. And, yes, he felt that Janice would take notice as well. However, she would not be in his department hereon. Not only that, but little did he know that those who on the surface were trying to be helpful to him were plotting his demise behind the scenes. Included in the deception was a plan to take some of his work and create errors, and then charging said errors back to him. But the one who instigated this chose to vacate for now, as negotiations that require a delicate touch were best postponed for a day or two.

As a contract employee Bruce did not have access to the company email. This alone aided and abetted the shroud of secrecy attached to the plot against him. It also required Janice to take care when answering in-house emails because tact and diplomacy might not be plentiful.

Drained by secret events, Bruce was in a state of mind and body where energy and enthusiasm to participate in a hectic night of socializing may be limited, and the lure of the couch and the television would prove very tempting.

83

ALTHOUGH HE TRIED AS best he could to feign a sense of togetherness, Bruce was all shook up by the obvious about-face where Janice was concerned. He was stuck on her beyond belief, and it showed despite his best efforts. Because he sensed betrayal, his angst was even more pronounced. He may not have been aware of the poison mouthpieces, but in his mind there were things he felt were not quite right. For sure there was nothing constructive about these developments.

Robin could be nice toward him at times, and at others could make him look like a clown. The workload had gotten heavier, to the point that things were often backed up a lot. He said to Paula one day that he hoped things could get back to normal. Robin jumped all over this, assuming it to be a wish for a return to the days of being sent home early some days. This wasn't really the case, but that was how she took it, as if it were a personal affront to her.

It was a beautiful morning as Janice made her way to work—one on which you could look through any window and see the reflection of the sunlight. This was a starred time to plan some redecorating around her new work station. Still on needles and pins where Bruce is concerned, she has mixed feelings on this saga. Part of her is glad she won't be his lead anymore, while on the other hand she will miss his way with words. For now she will be too busy to give this a whole lot of thought.

This applies off-duty as well as on, as she aims to finish up wintertime do-it-yourself projects, or spruce up the backyard as she gets ready to entertain in the comfort of her own home. She would give some serious consideration to having an addition built on her family home. If that does not prove possible, she might take to doing some redecoration to improve living conditions. In an urban neighborhood there is not much room for expansion, but at times she dreams of having the space, such as adding the pool or patio that she has always dreamed of having.

Having the impression that she might open up a little more now that she is in a different department, Bruce would try to engage Janice in conversation when both were in the break room. But her response was curt. "What'd I say?" she responded. "Unless it has to do with the job at hand, we're not going to go there." Bruce was stunned by this, but felt that he needed to keep on the move in order to prevent gloomy thoughts or irritability.

Janice would do the same as well, as a long public or social meeting, last-minute changes, and activities of youngsters would have her on the go, which can be good because being alone for too long is not recommended in the fragile condition she is currently in. She knows that Bruce was hoping she could be his. Everybody experiences such fragility now and then, but at this time it is very acute for both of them, each in their own way.

84

MENTAL ENERGY REMAINS STRONG for Bruce, but rational thinking proves elusive. If he could keep his temper and agitation under control, intellectual and physical accomplishments could be numerous. However, from an emotional standpoint he has been a nervous wreck. He actually cried when he learned that Janice was transferring out of the department. The woman who took over as lead is okay in his view but feels he could never come close to having the same kind of rapport that he did with Janice before the crash following his confession. As the focus swings toward analyzing this working relationship, there is some potential for conflict not only with her but also with other department members unless someone decided to be the peacemaker, and hopefully the person who takes on that role will be one who could bring the two of them to the bargaining table. At present there seems to be no one with the mindset of wishing for this to happen.

In his room that night Bruce was sullen and forlorn, beleaguered by thoughts that some of those around him would assume that his feelings toward Janice were only make believe. When consulting with a trusted friend on the phone, the caution he received was that if strain has become more noticeable in his committed workplace environment, he would need to take swift action to stem the negative flow.

Janice was to find her mood heading the opposite way as a surprise after lunch break, but on this day she felt the need to check her personal email on one of the computers located in the break room, and much to her surprise found one from a man she had a torrid affair with a while back. They had been out of touch for some time, but she was glad all over to get this email. At the time of the affair she felt as if she had found her straight shootin' cowboy.

Learning the ropes of her new position usually left Janice no time for non-work related chitchat. But the sense of excitement following the surprise email led her to exception. Tommy Burke is the man's name, and Kathy, the older woman who worked next to her in the other department and is now a steady visitor to her new department, was familiar with the scenario as they knew each other before working together. "He tells all the girls he's a cowboy," Kathy reminded Janice. She tells the story of how Tommy was at one time set to marry a girl named Sally. He broke off the engagement on very short notice, dropping her like a hot potato. "This man may get you sailing on a sea of love," Kathy continued, "but he will leave you marooned with no way to safety. For your sake, please don't get yourself involved. My dad was the love cowboy type as well. He was bad to my mama and no doubt others as well. Jan, you are too smart of a woman to fall for someone like this."

Kathy also kept whispering in Janice's ear concerning Bruce. She had suspicions about him too, and would do whatever she could to foil attempts to connect with whom she described as the white cowboy. At first not much attention was paid, but then she became convinced, and she along with George and Gloria from another office, were influential in turning her against Bruce. Now the email from Tommy was muddying the waters even more. Her dad having been the love 'em and leave 'em type made Kathy quite prejudiced in this regard. She would literally knock on wood in hope that she could pull enough strings so that Bruce would never get to socialize with Janice away from work.

85

WITH THE CALENDAR TICKING toward warmer weather, Janice now began wearing skirts more often. She still occasionally returned to the department where Bruce worked, as she needed to obtain information from some of the folks in that area. He muddled through the day feeling like the nowhere man. He would do his own share of knocking on wood in the hope that Janice would become friendlier to him again. Down to the wire he would strive to do his best work in hopes that he would soon reunite with Janice in spirit at least.

Dressed in light colors to hint of warmer days, Janice was good to go and in rare form. High spirits are likely to be in evidence as she begins this day. Her original ideas and plans for managing her new work area should be appreciated by other people. She was only this buoyant once in a blue moon, or so it seemed. It was ironic since she had so much on her mind away from the job as well as on it. With the weather now milder, she would now follow through with creative plans to improve the ambience, comfort, and value of her home. With her father's condition deteriorating to the point where death may not be far away, inheritance, tax, and insurance matters may require attention, and a family member advised her that it just might be wise to get these issues out of the way as early as possible. So she would heed this advice and would take one morning off from the job and get a lawyer's appointment to discuss all of these issues and get them off the table until the time actually arrives.

With mental stimulation remaining enhanced, a good mystery novel or TV show would help her switch off this evening and improve her overall sense of well-being. The one bit of morbidity dogging her was concerning Kathy's confession of what her email friend Tommy was all about. A part of her was hoping that she had a special angel to watch over her, and that as part of a couple she can and would benefit from today's stars by sharing happy rapport and companionship.

At one time she also did possess a rather strong attraction to Bruce, until her coworkers suddenly urged her to put a stop to it. This was shortly before he came clean with her, after which she told him to put a stop to it as well. This was done somewhat reluctantly, as she valued him as a worker. But he still isn't fully aware that his days on this job will soon be numbered. The plot against him has manifested itself full fathom, with five people doing everything they can to undermine him in ways he would probably not be able to easily decipher.

First there was George, the one-time supervisor of another department who got demoted over prior incidents as a sworn ladies' man who obviously also had a sweet spot for Janice as well. He, together with his office mate Gloria, who also had a lot of contempt for him although she knows little about him other than what she has heard. Kathy, the woman who brought Janice into the fold originally, has him pegged as a kind of dog who would be no good for her. Yet much of her prejudice in this regard stems from her growing up years with a skirt-chasing father.

Matt, the production manager of the facility, and the one who dictates the work priorities, is the fourth culprit. He has also developed much prejudice against Bruce, and has now documented much on paper which he feels could be used against him. Matt's assistant, a woman named Ariel, seems to have a whole aria sung which she feels could amount to a harassment case, even though by itself expressing an attraction isn't enough to qualify. What she thinks she has hurts his cause just the same.

86

A VARIED COUPLE OF days was now in store for concerned parties—some would be pleasant, some not so. For Janice attention continues to focus on fiscal matters. This was a good time to reassess her investments, her retirement plan, or possible stock options with her current employer. An old friend of hers, Brenda, has offered her the chance to partner up with her in the beauty supply business. She probably will join her at least part-time, and may have to confer with someone who works collecting debts or making loans. The sound advice this person could give should be able to arm them with ways to bring in the dollars more successfully. In addition, a debt owed by a friend would now be repaid, although this was done reluctantly. One day she loaned some money to a fairly close neighbor of hers who was down and out and needed to buy food to feed her children. Still in dire circumstances, Janice had to cajole her a bit for repayment, but just yesterday she heard someone knocking at the door, and it was her and she paid up.

Changes that occur now can be beneficial, so she would consider all of her options carefully to ensure that she would make the best choice. Problems can be resolved as the easy link between the most obvious and the unexpected incites actions that turn difficult situations into minor obstacles. This applies most earnestly to Janice's episode concerning Bruce. She is no longer his lead, and therefore does not have to even say hello to him if she doesn't care to. A part of her wanted to run from the situation while another was not so sure. Rumors have circulated that Bruce wants her to be his girl. Since this did not come out of his mouth these rumors cannot be substantiated, and could be a way to stir up the pot, as there were a bunch of folks that really want him out.

At the turn of the season the atmosphere for Bruce would turn as well. He would not mention Janice out loud, most likely in hope that others would feel that any attraction for her had subsided. The season to refrain from embracing seemed likely to last forever.

Bruce now would muddle through each Saturday and Sunday not knowing what to make of things. By now he felt as though the workplace atmosphere would never be the same now that Janice was no longer sitting across from him. He had no plans, however, for changing jobs as long as a sliver of hope existed for her to warm up again. Maybe, just maybe, something could develop now that she is out of his department. He now needed her presence as much as ever. He just wasn't being vocal about it. Anna, the woman who helped train him when he first arrived, was the one he would ask questions of most if he needed help on how to perform a task. He didn't get into his feelings for Janice with her as much as he did with some others. But now she could serve as his prime source of information, as she is now Janice's main contact in the department, the one with whom she would need to confer with in relation to her new duties. She was, however, quite a reserved person, not prone to getting involved with non-work related issues.

Like so many times before, Janice would play the ignore game when trying to acknowledge her whenever he would spot her. Memories would linger of when they shared casual banter in a friendly way. Her attitude toward him now was killing his soul.

87

THE LEAD POSITION IN Bruce's area has been taken over by a middle-aged woman named Lea. Unlike Janice, she is quite serene and soft spoken; not a practical joker. And while he does consider her a nice enough person, he is sure that the type of rapport he had with Janice could not be repeated. So he would do his best to do his job as hard as he could in the hope that it could help him in working his way back to Janice. His goal could be to get himself in line for a promotion into Janice's new department. Meanwhile, the folks who were determined to bring him down were acting like Santa Claus on Christmas Eve—making their list of points against Bruce, then checking it twice to make sure these points would stick should they be challenged. While it's not unusual for one to take a dislike to a fellow coworker, a mass betrayal of this magnitude is. What is likely to break loose is a plot that even a seasoned novelist might have some difficulty creating.

As much as he would attempt to practice restraint, Bruce would have tears on his pillow in the morning. He had grown quite depressed over the obvious demise of his working relationship with Janice. It was even harder on days when he thought she was looking real fine, which now happened more with the milder weather. Idealistic ideas and plans might now seem strange to other people but for Bruce this was the time to make dreams happen. He just couldn't show it while he was at work. But to himself every day he seemed to love Janice more and more. However, he would avoid for now making any life-changing decisions. As Anna, the woman he usually goes to for solving work-related issues, merges more into his work life, he may now feel more comfortable asking her what may be going on and why Janice is not paying attention to him when he does see her. She was of the opinion that it was just that she had a lot on her mind with the department transfer. But unlike others, she knows little of her personal life.

Now Bruce's logical side merges with the inspirational. Never one at a total loss for words, the artist within him is likely to emerge, bringing creative juices to the fore. Often people may be intimidated by Janice's highly unlikely combination of magnetism and sharp tongue, but when the workload was lighter she was more likely to be accommodating and open. It was during this period that his attraction toward her had first developed. But once it reached the boiling point the workload once again increased beyond the level it was at when he started. At these times she expected those working under her to behave like soldiers. He did not wish to see that side of her return and it is for this reason that he would make the extra effort to please her, and why he would perform such niceties as opening doors, etc.

Bruce would now take to listening to music and writing some new lyrics based on his experience with Janice. He would possibly consider having a demo made of one of them set to music.

He would go to the library and search the Internet in hopes of finding a performing venue where he could read a few of his works out loud. Or attending a concert could provide special pleasure as he was seeking relief from everyday duties and responsibilities. And then he would let himself drift into a fantasy world. He wondered how long he must continue to dream of Janice, knowing he only wanted to be with her.

88

IT WAS GETTING TO be an especially tricky time for Bruce. Morning trends are not overly supportive, but some improvement does arrive with each passing hour. It was lovely weather for early spring, and he thought how nice it would be to go for a walk or ride with Janice. But employment duties not only required him to snap to attention, but also would require her to end up spending considerable time on the phone or exchanging emails with folks from a distance. She now had her own work area with a phone, something she did not have when she was in the area Bruce occupies.

Meanwhile George, the man who for the most part instigated the plot to destroy Bruce, was up to more dirty work. Gloria, his usual assistant, was off for a few days, so he got Rosemary, who was her replacement, to check over some of the work of the operators. In particular he wanted her to doctor up some of the work Bruce did and create errors which could be charged against him and put them on Paula's desk.

Denise, one of the other people gathering information, once confessed to having a crush on Bruce even though she never made it obvious. She went into the new department along with Janice, but helped out elsewhere at times too. She was recruited for the plot against Bruce, but would find excuses not to be a link on what she referred to as a "chain of fools". They were miffed at being rebuffed in this effort by her, but had no authority by which they could sabotage her job. She couldn't understand why they would want to get their kicks by crafting such a plot to undermine him in this way. As a result, she was accused of attempting to cover up for him, but such was not the case at all. She personally hoped that this would all be uncovered one day in the hope that they would find themselves on the outside looking in. And who would be sorry then? She could have been the silent partner in this, but respectfully declined. This sent George through the roof, as he was adamant that this had to be done.

By the end of the day Bruce was pretty well worn down from the heavy workload. But so was Janice, who now wondered if the move to the new department was worth the aggravation. Things were not happening quite in the way she had anticipated. Arranging an upcoming vacation itinerary could be a thrill as she is anticipating getting away. She was scheduled to be off the week that her girls have their spring break, but she voluntarily cancelled that, as she has so much to do to set things up in this new work area. She also wondered what it would be like if she fell for Bruce. For a while she seemed to be headed there only to be pulled away by the dynamic of her position. Venus, the goddess of love, beauty, and money, is very much on her mind. And in fact she is wondering what Bruce is doing tonight. But any thoughts of extra-curricular activity must head into reverse mode until April 17, the deadline she was given to get her new area fully set up.

While Bruce considered himself a fortunate one to have a job at a time when many didn't, his star was rapidly fading out. Rumors of the supposed romantic link between him and Janice were spreading, bringing forth relationship issues that even she didn't realize existed. Efforts to pull the two of them apart were behind the recruiting of Janice to move from her former area into the new department. She had made Bruce so very happy by her presence when she was on her good game, and the drift was that the reverse may have been true as well. Matt, the production manager, solicited her services for the new department specifically out of desire to split her and Bruce up. He began to lay part of the blame on her as well, and then conditions and harmony on the job scene would deteriorate, and a promised pay increase for Janice, in addition to promotion to permanent status for Bruce, would be further delayed. It seemed as if he had stooped to the level of making a monkey out of Janice as well as Bruce.

89

CAUTION WAS NOW THE name of the game for both Bruce and Janice, each in their own way. A large number of circumstantial trends are impacting on the weekend activities. Bruce would try to pace all of his activities as best he could. As his vitality diminishes, giving up would seem easier than making an effort. By moving slowly he felt that he might lessen the chance of quickly becoming overwhelmed by obligations or what he perceives as limitations on his life. A task that requires concentration or creative flair can keep his mind fully and hopefully pleasantly occupied. He had begun writing a story about a veteran who returned from combat only to develop a debilitating disease, and he chose to spend a good share of the weekend by putting more words to paper.

Because his morale was down as well he would also need to take extra care of his health so that he would not develop a tendency to succumb to infections or viruses, thus becoming too weak to fight. He is now convinced that a battle may very well lie ahead of him.

He is becoming more aware of the toxic atmosphere at his workplace. In its own way it is every bit as toxic as certain liquids and chemicals. Deceptive trends prevail, warning Bruce to beware slick coworkers selling a bill of goods which may not be at all accurate. And that included the woman who occupied the space right next to his.

Robin was often friendly toward Bruce, but lately she had learned of a permanent job opening. She wanted to be sure that Bruce didn't get it, and as a result joined the brigade of those who wanted to bring him down. She somehow assumed that he had been taking on the role of eager beaver, and therefore she would begin the efforts to assault his character based on his obvious feelings toward Janice. Matt, the production manager, was the one who tipped Robin off. He, too, was quite prejudiced against Bruce and had the authority to make a move toward his ouster. He also wanted to do all he could to see that he never returned.

90

IT WAS NOT A good morning for Bruce, as sensitive trends were to continue. He had been lonely too long for Janice to at least warm up to him a little bit, but it never seems to have happened. Despite repeated attempts at telling himself that it's all right, he knew very well that this was not the case. He now would liken himself to the Shakespearian character Prospero, adrift on the sea surrounded by water. The angst over the situation now seemed to spread like a cancer through the food chain. Important relationships and friendships would all seem rocky, and he would need to work extra hard to cultivate any level or warmth and understanding. These feelings were only intensified by what he perceived as a continued raunchy attitude toward him on the part of Janice. Yet with the exception of Robin, his next door workmate, the rest of the conspirators seemed determined not to let on that anything was out of the ordinary.

A combination of feelings of isolation and negative thoughts would continue to fester unless he was surrounded by family or friends helping to maintain his spirits and a sense of good humor. As an only child whose parents had passed on, he had no real family left. He really doesn't want to involve Laura, the woman he sometimes sees, in all of this. So this leaves him to deal with the situation as best he can. In a conversation with an acquaintance one day he began to tell the story of how he fell for this woman who was his lead person at the job and how everything crashed upon coming clean about it. The response he got was that if the habits or behavior of someone he works with are now straining patience, be sure to hold your tongue for a little longer or you might say more than you intended. The acquaintance was only the messenger, and Bruce stated that he wouldn't direct anger that way for whatever results ended up coming down.

When Matt, the production manager, slips into Bruce's work area he froze up, determined to remain fixated on what he was doing. He was one of those who was trying to find what he could in order to undo his tenure there. Bruce was still unaware as to whether he or any of the others, including Janice, were devil or angel. For although Janice still had the ability to ignite his pleasure zone, Bruce did not have good vibrations when it came to her being on his side.

In free moments Bruce would shift his passion as best he could, increasing his intellectual interest in all things consisting of a creative nature. He learned of a dance for singles while he was online at the library. When he arrived home he got dressed, hit the expressway and headed to the dance. Perhaps he would meet someone who could leave him breathless. He is likely to be attracted to someone who could provide mental stimulation as well as excitement.

91

AT THE DANCE BRUCE met a lady with whom he shared a few dances. One of the songs was a classic titled, "The More I See You." Although he found this lady attractive, he couldn't help but think about Janice while that song was playing. It turned out to be a frustrating evening after all because this lady declined any further contact for reasons unbeknownst to him. All she told him was that she may see him again at a future dance. He didn't even learn her name.

Just when he thought life was improving, more pressure comes along to push his patience and resolve to the limit. At a meeting he learned that his work was being monitored more closely than ever. To him this was a subtle sign that the hand of fate may be closer to knocking at his front door. However, if anyone can rise to the occasion it is Bruce. At least that is the way he is thinking, sure that he can work it out in a way that would ensure that he could conquer whatever form of adversity came his way.

Not too long ago he by chance caught Janice in the hallway when nobody else happened to be around. To himself he thought this might be a chance to reconcile, but he passed it up and said nothing out of fear that it could make things worse rather than better. Getting along with his coworkers may be difficult, so it would be wise for him to keep a low profile at the moment.

To relieve the stress of changing conditions Bruce would take a scenic ride after work this day. Little did he know the deception that would be in store for him on the following day. Janice was dressed very sharp with a stunning blue dress on. Around ten o'clock all the keyers in his department were called off, having been told that the system would be down for about an hour, perhaps more. The way Janice was dressed that day put Bruce into one-track mind mode. Before long he would be mindful of just what the intended scenario was surrounding these events.

Never one to venture into the break and lunch room, this time Janice spent considerable time there, after which she spent time in another room standing right where Bruce could see her through the window chatting with other workers. His suspicion that this could be a set-up would be confirmed before too long. Gloria, George's assistant, walked over to where the department supervisor, Paula, was sitting. It appeared as if she was giving her some sort of information. He now had the foreboding feeling that something was up, and that he may not be returning to this job. The cruel nature of the day's events was confirmed when Bruce turned on his cell phone soon after his arrival home. Indeed his premonition that he would be gone proved to be accurate. Sherry called from Cadence Staffing to inform him that his assignment was finished and that he need not return the next day. Samantha, the account manager, was on vacation and Sherry substituted.

Bruce's dismissal was cause for those who organized against him to celebrate their victory. Even before his attraction to Janice became apparent, this group had felt the need to squelch his ambition though he really had no real desire for any higher position besides being added to the regular staff.

Meanwhile, as he was heading in toward the city that evening, it seemed quite apropos that "As Tears Go By" was playing on his car radio. He was originally planning to go in on the train, but he missed the train he wanted and didn't feel like waiting an hour for the next one. It was while he was at the platform that he checked his cell and got the dreaded message. This would color his world with gloomy shades as he was sure to have a hard time getting a new job in this down economy.

Were he not as level-headed he might end up hitching a ride with a stranger to God knows where.

Although obviously depressed by the sudden turn of events, Bruce was determined to hang tough and move on as best he could. Although adapting to change is not always easy for him, changing jobs, launching a keep fit program, or joining a special-interest club can now be beneficial. This way new people entering his life will be able to introduce more variety and excitement.

But Bruce would be forever changed and daunted as he learned through a psychic reader that he was clearly the victim of a pack of lies.

92

WITH PROFOUND INSIGHT BRUCE compared his situation to breaking up with an intense lover. Recovering from this will no doubt be hard to do. This unholy alliance of people, at least five and possibly up to seven in number, would often rave on as to what a detriment he was to the facility and operation. With insightful reading and his new free time he would attempt to develop the best scenario possible regarding what went down. With the spring planting season around the corner, he might consider ways in which to help his landlady make her garden grow, as this is one hobby she takes great pride in. And it would keep in check his tendency to want to mess around with so much free time unexpectedly on his hands. Not really sorry about his own actions at the workplace, he still is in a state of wondering if he would still have his job had he not come clean about his attraction to Janice. On this he may never know.

Bruce would have to deal with the cloud of suspicion now reigning over today's affairs, hoping his thoughts and words are powerful and are able to change and transform. With a suspicious mind plaguing his thoughts, he would head down to the local unemployment office to file his claim. Then he would head over to the computer area where he would promptly email thank you notes to both Janice and Paula, the department supervisor. This is something he had never done before, even after jobs which ended unceremoniously. But he was of the mindset that he wanted to open up some avenue of contact with Janice should she wish to get in touch at a future time, and felt that this would be the best way for him to do this. Then he would turn to sending out resumes for potential positions. He managed to send out ten of these when along came Mary, the supervisor of that area. She told Bruce that he would need to vacate the area as others were waiting.

Not really versed in such talents, Bruce thought over what he would say if making a public speech. This is something he might have to do one day should he choose to crusade for greater social justice for everyday people, which he is now more apt to do than ever if he were to become fortunate enough to make the right connections. Taking part in a debate or conducting a media interview could also be possible outlets for his passion. With proper practice, he should be delighted by the ease with which words roll off his tongue.

Leah Jones, a local news reporter, often deals in cases where the underdog has been mistreated or otherwise victimized. Most of the time these have to do with consumer rip-offs, but Bruce wondered to himself whether just maybe she might be willing to take a look at and possibly investigate his case. So he accessed her email through the TV station's website, wrote a description of events, and sent it off.

With the sudden upheaval now gripping his life, the cosmos were now prompting Bruce to start talking and take action in regard to current directions and future goals. He would begin the process of reassessing where he is now and also where he wants to be by the end of the year. While filing for unemployment and sending out resumes is a start, he has to hope that some of this will begin to bear fruit and soon. Yet in the back of his mind one of his main goals is for Janice to be part of his life at some level even if not in an intimate way. One day he would find her address and perhaps phone number on one of these people finder web sites. He would love to be able to spot her by chance while he was passing through her neighborhood on the way to somewhere. But that was as far as it would go—just some basic wishful thinking. He did not have any interest in ever driving by her house out of fear that this might mess up the case if he were successful.

One of Bruce's avocations was as a writer, and he was working on a new story when everything went down. With the suddenly new free time he now had, he should make steady progress. This would for sure be a great time to begin a novel, but first he would need to finish the one he is on now. His current dilemma would be great fodder for one, providing that he was able to learn the truth of the matter. It could also provide fodder as well for an academic thesis or research on the pitfalls of office politics and workplace mind games. But his circumstance also dictated that he would need to try to find a new work assignment as soon as he could. But he could not put this experience on his resume in order to avoid possible blacklisting. And he would also need to prepare himself for the chance that he may need to make confessions should he be challenged for unemployment benefits. Not coming clean would be foolish.

But he was haunted by the internal questioning as to whether having come clean with Janice was equally foolish on his part. At the time he felt it necessary in order to clear the air, but never thought the aftermath would be as stressful as it was. And at times it nearly moved him to tears.

93

ALTHOUGH DISTRAUGHT BY KNOWING that the woman he hoped could be the love of his life was here and now gone from his life, Bruce still put on a brave face in the hope that he would get lucky and be vindicated of any perceived wrongdoing. Still, he was reeling from the trauma of now once again being out of a job. He would do his best to look forward to a day when progress would be swift and easier to achieve. And he often dreamed of Janice, often visualizing being able to see her again.

Through a psychic reader he was able to ascertain that he fell the victim to some who had the venom of a cobra at their disposal, and used it. He was also told that Janice was as attracted to him as he was to her, but wedding bells were probably nowhere in their future. Any thought of a relationship between them was squelched by those who were jealous both of the situation at hand and of Bruce's organizational talents, which they felt threatening.

With the monkey already on his back, Bruce faced a long struggle trying to move forward. On the Monday morning following his discharge, he was on the computers at the local unemployment office. Much to his surprise, upon checking his email he saw one supposedly from Janice. When he opened it up he found a note which said "Please leave me the hell alone! Don't send me any more emails!" Upon closer examination he discovered that there were four or five unrelated contacts from his list who supposedly received this same email. It would now be quite apparent that the monkey would remain on his back for some time to come. The great voice within him urging him to move forward now entwines with the jealousy of those responsible for his downfall, making for a strange brew. If there was ever a time when he needed the force of an angel to watch over him, it was now. But such fortune would be more elusive than he could ever have imagined.

No angel was to be found that was capable of sending lots of good luck and cheer his way. Because of the down economy he would need to make the most of the opportunities presented. There was nowhere to run, and he knew it. This became even more obvious when Samantha, the representative of Cadence, got wind of the email which was sent out in his name. Despite all the effort he put into telling her that he was not responsible for that particular email, she would not buy it. Eventually he told her that he was going to fight to prove he did not send it and then the donnybrook ended. At the end of the day he felt more depressed than he had in ages, yet determined to prove his innocence. He would feel a whole lot better if he was able to gain ground on an attempt to set the record straight. He would find this to be a much more difficult battle than he envisioned. Above all he wished that Samantha would be gone from the picture.

In spite of it all Bruce would do his best to hang on. And though he never thought of himself as one who is prone to such, what leadership skills he had were put to the test, although a team effort could advance under his guidance. Thus there were some who saw him as a potential threat to their future. And to stop this they would begin to dig, determined to ascertain just how much sugar Bruce was heaping upon Janice. As it was, in the final few weeks of his tenure what lemonade had been made had been turned back into lemons. The old adage that one can get farther with sugar than vinegar was turned on its head. In Janice's mind Bruce might as well have been a stranger, because that was how she behaved toward him. For his part he believed that everything that went on was behind the scenes. And yet there were those who felt that the scapegoating was wrong. That included Denise, the assistant in another area who had been dragged into this plot unintentionally.

Now with no job and no good leads for a new one, Bruce now knew that pleasure would have to come from people who could make his world a little bit brighter. But if a new relationship does develop somewhere along the way, it would likely prompt him to show how much he cared for this person. He might even be prompted to send a bouquet of flowers to his lover, or purchase a stuffed animal for someone near and dear to him. But for now he would just have to dream on, as with no new income he could not be fortunate enough to be able to do it. He is now in reality that his world has sunk like quicksand, dropping him into the throes of despair.

When in the city one day he did meet a nice woman at a bus stop. They chatted quite a while and did exchange phone numbers. And yet he knew he would have to get to know her quite a bit better before actually making any commitment. She would very likely fly off on him like a bird. He has been there before.

Later in the day after returning home from his solo excursion he would set aside some time in which to be alone with his thoughts. In happier times he might have felt like going dancing, but now, if he got too bored at home, he might choose to take a walk and commune with nature.

94

A COUPLE OF WEEKS later would find Bruce in a more tranquil frame of mind. He would even look up on the roof of the house where he loves to see and hear the spring birds chirping. A more soothing mood arrives along with more benign weather conditions as the morning sun moves through the sky. He is for the most part a peace-loving, likeable individual. Yet at the same time, however, the golden sun merging with erratic clouds within his unsetting mind produces a restless attitude urging him to be out and about rather than remaining at home. But now with no job he would not have the means to go out and about in the style he had grown accustomed to.

At his former workplace Paula, Bruce's department's main supervisor, was summoned by an associate of one of the perpetrators of the plot against him. Wondering and puzzled by what this could be about, she was hesitant at first but once she finished what she was doing she heeded the call.

Annie, a petite woman who worked in the same office as the two assumed ringleaders, George and Gloria, asked Paula if she wanted to know a secret. Really not totally in the affirmative, she was still curious so she told Annie to lay it on her. And she proceeded to tell Paula that George had been told that Bruce was not guilty of any type of harassment toward Janice. As he was himself interested at one time, and aware of his prowess as a ladies' man, she declined to get involved. "On his end a sense of love and warmth continues," Annie went on. "So not wanting to do the dirty work himself, he ably recruited Gloria to advise Janice not to have much to do with Bruce and only speak to him if there was something she needed to tell him regarding the particular job at hand. If you were to ask me, I would say that he was a fool to go as far as he did in his effort to get him ousted. This was a very unfair activity, and I wish it had been in my power to have aborted this plot."

Shocked as she was by Annie's daunting revelation, Paula nevertheless chose to keep silent out of fear of saying something stupid that could get her in trouble. Longing to somehow get in touch with him to set the record straight, she knew that, for the time being at least, her hands were tied.

While it was also a cloud over Janice, she chose to exhibit fortitude from moving on. For her this would be a good day to surprise her loving daughters by booking a weekend retreat or possibly arranging a business trip to include above all a few extra days that loved ones can take part in and share happy memories. She has put in a bid on a different job within the company. If considered, it would require a journey to the corporate headquarters. But the extras could only happen if it were to occur during the girls' summer break and if she could enlist a responsible adult to stay with the girls during the time she is at meeting.

An old song said that fools rush in where wise men never go. With that in mind Bruce would now question his own wisdom where his having fallen for Janice was concerned. He feels it may very well not have lasted should anything have developed. A veteran of a couple of social groups he was active in during younger years, he had developed a reputation as one of these lovers who wander. However, somehow he wasn't sure that was wholly justified. In launching his social life, his parents advised him that he should make a friend out of one of the guys who could be a cog in the wheel of introducing him to girls. The crux of this advice was that spending time with someone he considered a mentor, whose opinions and experience he could respect, could be very worthwhile and informative. Little did he know that the one he chose, whose name was Pete, proved to be one who steered him in the direction of wanderlust. His philosophy was to date as many as you can and get as much as you can out of each one.

The one defense Bruce has when it came to this association was that it occurred during that hedonistic time frame after The Pill and before AIDS, when it was so widely assumed that remaining footloose and having as few responsibilities as possible was the way to go. And in many ways, as much as the world around him had changed, he has for the most part stuck with this mindset. Presently lacking a suitable mentor to use some friendly persuasion on him, Bruce for the most part will need to go it alone in dealing with the true extremity of his disappointment.

95

NOW QUESTIONING WHETHER HE even had the right to show any affection toward Janice, Bruce now contemplated what his next move should be. He wanted to get back to Janice so much that he could hardly bear it. Wouldn't it be nice, he thought, if he could just spend some time with her even if the contact just amounted to talking? And, of course, getting some insight as to what went down and why.

When he woke up he was reminded when he turned on the radio that it was Friday the 13th. But he felt fine, and was certain that there was nothing to fear from today's date, except perhaps being late for getting wherever he might need to go because current stormy weather conditions and patterns urge him to remain in bed a little longer this morning. But because he needed to get down to the unemployment office he knew it wasn't possible to do so. So he would at least proceed at a steady pace without rushing around, which could hinder rather than help progress.

Yesterday Bruce saw Linda, his claim representative at the unemployment office. His claim for benefits was being challenged by Cadence Staffing on the premise that he was in fact discharged for what they deemed to be inappropriate behavior. He chose to file an appeal, and arrived at the office too late to meet with her. So he was to return today and was encouraged to arrive around the time the claims office opened. Linda would ask him to give her a few details, and when he gave his account she said to him "Don't let go. This has really got to you, and you deserved to be treated fairly." She then advised him that he did have the right to the free services of an attorney to help him explain his case. She was confident that the eventual verdict would go in his favor, but had to tell him that the decision would not be in her hands. Having proclaimed his innocence and having Linda's support made him feel just a little bit better, but not enough to lift the fog altogether.

Behind-the-scenes work may now keep Bruce occupied, as he would need to rehearse what he would say at the hearing once it comes about. He chose to enlist the services of an attorney, but her only obligation was to call the day before the hearing to explain the case. In the meantime he had just one serious job offer, but heard nothing further following the original interview.

It would be several weeks before the scheduled hearing date arrived. It was to be conducted over the phone as opposed to being held in person. The case would be decided by a non-partisan judge based on evidence by all concerned parties. Samantha, the account manager for Cadence Office Staffing, was to represent them, and Bruce and the attorney representing him. When Cadence was called, a woman told them that Samantha was not there. She said that she was out sick, and the hearing as a result was a draw, and the moderating judge indicated that a rematch might take place.

The rhythm of the rain was pounding rather hard when Bruce got off the phone following what he often referred to as the hearing that wasn't. Because Samantha was a no-show, no explanation of the facts was presented, which could prove to be a liability. Although it was now the end of June, the area was mired in cool, cloudy and rainy conditions at a time of year when it is usually hot and humid. The possible deception would prove good timing for the weather at the moment. This actually would be satisfactory since he would now prefer solitude rather than interacting with strangers or even casual friends. Even personal projects that are dear to his heart, such as his prose and poetry writing, would be pushed to the side as he would now be content to just watch the world go by. His days of being pegged as one of these lovers who wander were now behind him. It was virtually impossible to go back there now if for no other reason than that the money is lacking for him to even come close to that sort of lifestyle. His whole life was now a drag on his existence.

There would now be outstanding chores waiting for attention, which could benefit if he were to be determined to complete unfinished tasks instead of beginning anything new or complex. But he would need to put whatever he could to the side as his main goal was the need to find new employment. With Janice no part of his life now, he was in need of being back on the street looking for work and remembering when.

96

ALTHOUGH UNSUCCESSFUL SO FAR in finding new work, Bruce would soon find a smooth landing of sorts. He felt as though vindication would come his way shortly. In reading of a psychic nature he was told that it was some jealous people at his former workplace who told Janice to tell him no and that this was really not her doing. Physical resources should be good as the weather glides toward improvement after the unusual conditions of the past couple of days. Valerie, an agent at the unemployment office, assured him that his case was being reviewed and that an answer should be forthcoming. Following this he would spend time doing a job search on their computers.

Through his own readings he was told that Robin, the woman the next work station over from him, was one of the conspirators against him. She seemed to have an unstable sort of personality to begin with. No doubt she did have a lot of things to think about due to health issues. But she still didn't have to be so mean.

There was a suspicion that his popularity was about to rise by leaps and bounds, so Robin should not have been surprised if people were to demand more of his attention. After all, Robin herself often solicited his knowledge on how to do a procedure when none of the key people were there. She got wind of some possible permanent position opening up, and that would be an incentive for her to turn against Bruce since he seemed to be a logical candidate for it. And like him she was on loan from Cadence, and had stated that she was not at all fond of Samantha, the manager of this account. If he had known all this he would have done his best to try and change her mind. She was a sort of Jekyll and Hyde, who could be almost loving at one time yet so cruel and cutting at other times. She sensed that his popularity was about to rise by leaps and bounds, so she was not surprised that people were to demand more of his attention. This irked Robin even though she was among those who sought him out. She had a jealous bone over this.

Sensing that time won't let her wait, when Matt, the facility production manager, informed her that there could be an opening soon, she jumped on the bandwagon. She then learned of the plot to have Bruce ousted, and she jumped aboard ship for the sole reason that she wanted to see to it that she got the job she was after, but she eventually found herself on the outside looking in. This was because her fragile health condition led to too much unscheduled time off.

Did Janice feel that it was a wonderful world now that Bruce was no longer part of her life? Probably not, although she felt that while the quest for an affair was occurring she felt more uptight. But yet she had mixed feelings as to whether he really deserved to be fired. Like Robin, she also was somewhat of a Jekyll and Hyde who tended to go with whatever side her bread was buttered on. She was both relieved he was not around yet questioning of the result.

The first hint she had of Bruce's interest in her came a couple of weeks before his confession. A paperback writer of one self-published story, he gave her the privilege of looking through it. Although he told her that she could keep it, she returned it one day quite to his surprise. At the time she at least was nice to him, which would not be the case once he came clean.

But Janice was in a celebratory mood as she would be embarking on a vacation trip to another land, invited by a friend who had moved there. But if she were to go out on a shopping spree, she would need to be aware that it could wreak havoc with her budget. However, she certainly didn't wish to embark on her journey looking like a rag doll. Therefore, this could be a good time to take better care of her personal needs and to focus on what it is that makes her feel good to be alive.

She would now consider updating her hairstyle, getting a professional manicure, or buying the new pair of shoes that she has had her eye on.

After dong all of the above to prepare for her upcoming seven-day weekend, she would cram for a couple of hours and then plan to spend time with someone special this evening. The new man in her life, whose name is Ron, is one who treats her good yet still has a bit of the rough edge she claims to like. Yet because he has a reputation as a playboy, she will need to be on her guard and not get herself too deeply involved. But it will be a tough call. She doesn't know how he does what he does to her, but at present it seems good. He makes her forget the whole debacle with Bruce.

97

BEING IN AN INSPIRING mood, this would be another day for Janice to escape routine tasks and household chores and do whatever fits her fancy. Meeting friends for lunch or planning a special treat for the girls can be fine ways to relax and increase her emotional comfort.

Yet despite this upside to her life, memories of the whole affair concerning Bruce would not fade away. And as she has been stressed out over the last few weeks by constant arguments and discord both at work and within the family, she is glad that relief is in sight. She does still spend considerable time wondering whether she did the right thing by her tendency to just walk on by when she was near where Bruce was working without any attempt to acknowledge his presence. She would from time to time tell herself that it's all right to feel this way, to wonder if there were better ways in which she could have dealt with things. And if Bruce would still have his job if such was the case.

Now Marilyn, the traditional town crier type of her neighborhood who would like to be their lives' ruler, would approach Janice before she got the chance to move into the placid surroundings of home and her zone of relaxation. She was wondering how she was getting along with the new love in her life. "How does she know I have someone?" she asked herself. Not one who enjoys others meddling into her zone of love, pleasure, and creative pursuits, she tried to dodge any intimate details. She confessed that from now on she chose not to reply to such intrusions. However, she informed Marilyn that she met him back on April 22, and that it seems as if he is just her style. But Marilyn would not let Janice get away without informing her that this person is known to be quite the ladies' man. "Holy cow," Janice thought to herself. "How does she know so much?" At least she is certain that she does not know about Bruce. That obviously was because he was her coworker and never around the neighborhood.

Feeling pangs of guilt, Janice often confessed to herself that she was sorry for the dastardly ways in which she treated Bruce in his final days at her workplace. She wondered if he would accept her apology should they someday happen to reconnect. She felt as if she was the good witch in disguise as evil. Due to possible legal hassles, however, she has been counseled not to seek out any contact. She is now somewhat aware that the staffing agency which sent him there challenged his bid for unemployment benefits, but is unaware as to whether he has a lawyer. She wishes this drama would go away at great speed.

Not wishing to play the game of love within the workplace, she felt she had little choice but to turn the tables on Bruce and act as she did. This, however, was not entirely her choice. The deck was stacked against him, and bad karma could have grabbed her as well had she chosen not to cooperate with those who crafted the plot.

Needing desperately to put this sordid episode out of mind, this would be a starred period for Janice to explore the depths of her current romantic relationship and to spend more quality time with other favorite companions.

But the person who had the most reason to feel lack of power over this situation was the department head, Paula. Upon returning from vacation just before Bruce's dismissal, she found some errors attributed to him on her desk. Yet something told her that these could have been rigged. She already knew of the undercurrent that would push him out, and despite her best efforts to rescue him from this, it was to no avail and the decision was totally taken out of her hands. At busy times especially she wished he were still here because he was for the most part very proficient at his work and spotted problems upon occurrence. She retained some misgivings about the way things were handled, up to the point of having as little as possible to do with those who would bring him down.

While Paula would sympathize with Bruce's plight, she was hesitant to reach out to him for fear of putting her own job in jeopardy. This is something she may have to live with for the rest of her life.

98

FOLLOWING HIS VICTORY WITH the unemployment office, Bruce's life would be satisfactory for a time. Early morning vibes could at times be a little tricky, with money matters creating some negativity. He had just self-published a second book, but knows it will be a long time, if ever, before he sees any payout from this. He now was working on a third, this one featuring Janice as the central figure. Trying to put as much soul and sentiment into it as possible, it is a fiction story about what her life might be like. He imports himself into this story only briefly, just as a person passing through her life. At the same time he can't help himself as far as being wistful for what might have been. He now has his daily routine pretty well established. Around the time the staffing agency offices open, he will phone those he is registered with to inform them of his availability in the hope that he can shake things up a bit.

As the day passes, he feels the atmosphere improves as well as relations with those in close proximity to him. But at times he feels so alone and finds that he is apt to shed tears over having been taken for a clown over his interest in Janice. His obsession with her would simply not fade away, at least not for a while longer.

Midmorning on most days is an ideal time to walk to the library, at times talking with a passer-by or neighbor while on the way to be returning a borrowed possession from there. Now in the throes of the warm season, he would walk the three blocks there every day unless it was raining. Working with Janice had made him very happy for a while. Since this job and experience was yanked from him he has been struggling to find his way in this world. He is very disillusioned over folks at the workplace assuming that he was another one of these sweet talking guys who would only cause heartbreak.

Listening to music throughout the day can soothe and calm the senses. Indulging his romantic side has not been within his realm since the infatuation with Janice crashed. She was the one who piqued his senses, and is now numb to the idea of forming a new relationship, although he does still get together with Laura on occasion. On some evenings he finds himself tempted to go off somewhere just to chase away the blues. Going to a movie or a concert could appeal during the evening. Yet the majority of the time finds him passing on both fronts. He has been lonely too long, but doesn't feel that indulging in entertainment would benefit him that much since the distractions would not enable him to enjoy the scene. Until there was Janice there were other women who had his interest, and several times he had experienced the frustrations of being interested in those who for one reason or another did not or would not reciprocate.

Bruce would derive some satisfaction from coming in contact with those who would be out walking the dog. These days he feels as if the best way to obtain a friend is to buy a dog. He would recall that a one-time government official who later committed suicide had made this said statement.

His continued obsession over Janice and what went down at his workplace have been bad for him, and he is fully aware of this. Was he still making money he might be a shopper who would have a keen eye for quality and might pick up some extra-good bargains while browsing in upscale stores. But this is an aspect of life which has eluded him, and he now avoids this scene like the plague.

99

IT WAS NOW THE time of the season when the weather would be chancy, with the threat of severe thunderstorms often occurring in the aftermath of the day's heating. These atmospheric conditions related eerily to the storms occurring in Bruce's life. Now a full month has passed since he won his battle for unemployment benefits by default when Samantha turned out to be a no-show at the hearing. But this was negated by the fact that by this happening he was robbed of the chance to tell the true story of what actually occurred and of this account of what he feels went down and why he feels he was set up.

Another morning dawns when problems and concerns over money would put a damper on the day's activities. He knew he needed to find work as soon as possible, but nothing was coming forth. Once again he went through his roster of staffing agencies, but once again came up empty. It was at this point that he came up with a tantalizing idea.

By this time he would feel that he had been way too extravagant with his calls to psychic readers, some of which seemed to indicate that someday he and Janice would be together, and at the very least get the chance to meet and be able to set the record straight. Distraught that she never became his party doll, he tried in vain to come up with ways to seek some solace. He chose to phone Cadence Office Staffing to inform them that he had been cleared of any wrongdoing. He would walk tall, and tell them that as this was the case that they should clear his name as well, making him eligible at least for other opportunities even if not for being sent back to where Janice was, which he knew would be occupational suicide. Samantha happened to be the person he reached upon making the call. Nonetheless, upon relating this detail to her, she was not buying it. She curtly told him that the only reason he got off was because she had been out sick that day, and that she refused to work with him.

Feeling that Samantha was cavalier with the joint endeavor they were tangled up in, he promptly informed her that he was going to file a grievance and appeal with the corporate office of Cadence. Sensing some nervousness on her part, he promptly hung up the phone without waiting for response, knowing that doing so could create some discord. He would then be encouraged to hold off on further discussions of the matter until making the proper overture to the headquarters. But there was no doubt that Samantha's cavalier attitude toward him not only left his spirit in bits and pieces, but also left him wondering if she was a willing participant in the plot against him. During the course of his readings he was told that she was for the most part against having a male in that department. Could it be, he wondered, that he reminded her of someone from her past who may have wronged her in some way? At any rate, he knew there would be no sugar coming from her.

At the same time Bruce knew that he would need to reorganize his finances as the following week began. The day dawned sunny and bright; perfect for a daydream. But his new condition would force any daydreaming to the back burner. His landlady had suggested that he begin taking his Social Security as he was now old enough to do so. But on this particular day the urge to daydream won, and he would elect to hold off on financial discussions and decisions with anyone at least until later in the week.

On a recent excursion Janice and the girls would drive by a county fair which advertised pony rides. This intrigued the girls, and Jamicia in particular wanted to go ride one. But, just back from an excursion to the islands which proved quite expensive, she balked at the idea. She would refuse to give in to the fiscal demands of her children since she didn't have extra cash on hand. The pony rides by themselves weren't costly, but the whole fair experience would be.

But Jamicia was not satisfied, and she began pouting. These eyes of hers pleaded and begged, and this pleading eventually got to her. Finally Janice told her that if she cleaned up her room and the kitchen and then take the garbage out that they could go to the fair and ride the ponies—the latter as long as proper supervision was provided on site so she would not fall off.

Bruce just received his latest unemployment check, and upon returning from the bank and paying his landlady the rent one of his housemates asked him if he had some extra money. But he told him that he couldn't spare any. Even if he did have money to spare, this was not a good time to make a loan even to a friend or associate, especially if they don't have a reliable track record of repaying loans in the past. And while he has no idea what this person's track record is, he recalls having been burned in the past, and chose to decline the risk.

100

WITH THE MEMORY OF being burned by the betrayal of this job along with the image of Janice still fresh on his mind, this would be a trying time for Bruce. Despite all the resumes he has sent out, no work prospects were forthcoming. He now wondered if feeling confident was something he would now experience just once in a blue moon. A tense atmosphere now prevails as he awaits word on his appeal to Cadence Staffing's corporate headquarters, although there should be a few lucky highlights to increase enjoyment of the day. These mostly amount to having the time to enjoy the good weather while it is here. He would like to go off and be wild for a time, but the combo of financial restraints and excessive worry conspire to prevent this.

Wishing he could get a message to Janice would occupy much of his time. He wonders if she really would be one to stand by him in order for the record to be set straight, as his principal psychic reader had told him. So far no one has come forward.

As a feeling of being overwhelmed has threatened to torpedo activities, he now wished he could talk over problems with someone who may be more resourceful in clearing away obstacles. The psychic readings started becoming too costly to keep doing as regularly as he had been. One escape mechanism he would use was to buy a ticket to ride on a train into the center of the big city to observe the action, trying to clear away the debris left by all those who would mess with his soul and his ability to continue to earn a living. His one hope he is clinging to is that he can get some answers through the appeal process. And while some of the urges had by now worn off, there were still times when he would want Janice as bad as ever, frustrated in knowing that there wasn't a single thing that he could do about it. He could have his pick of the litter were he better situated, but only Janice would be able to fill his senses with the feelings that have eluded him for the bulk of his life with the exception of a few fleeting romances.

Not knowing when or even if he would be successful in getting relief, Bruce decided to research websites dedicated to workplace issues. He found this one site, and signed up, counting himself in. Or he may assume that role by taking someone under his wing and passing on his own knowledge and insights. That is, if he should have the fortune of connecting with a community of folks who have shared experiences and could unite in a common cause.

With tricky mind games having done him in challenging his very being, coupled with limiting spending power due to prolonged unemployment, creative ideas and motivation would be in short supply. He would spend some time at the library—other than that he would just watch the days go by, hoping to catch the break he really needs. This would limit productivity as he would require inspiration in order to perform daily activities. He wished he could slip away somewhere on holiday, but such a luxury is not in the cards.

101

RESTFUL, HUSH-FILLED NIGHTS ARE a rarity for Bruce at present. But for a change he managed to break this pattern, and as a result decided he needed to get busy if indeed he were to ever become well-respected again. An action-packed day would be in store for him despite the limited resources he must now contend with. He elected to take his Social Security benefit to be able to at least have some cash flow. If nothing, it would be enough to prevent him from ever having to be back on the street. He now wants to think of his interests again, yet all the same remembering when he felt he could be on top of the world working with Janice.

It was a beautiful morning, and he tried to master the attitude to match despite all the pitfalls. His traditional life patterns are now in conflict with his modern life demands. He would be one to confess that he finds the explosion of technology daunting, much of which he currently has no wish for, often longing for the simpler life of earlier times when life seemed easier.

What perplexed him most about the thwarting of a potential romance with Janice was that through history many have met and even married as a result of meeting at work. Bruce pointed out the example of his own parents, and Tim, the second-shift person whom Janice jokingly referred to as her boyfriend, had mentioned that his parents met that way as well. But there were times when she would act like the queen of whatever, and the period following his confession left him constantly wondering just how much she was swayed to turn against him by do-gooders. Then he would take to contemplating just what route he should take in order to get the answers to this.

He would take to doing a lot of walking both to get exercise and save energy, running only the necessary errands by car. So his energy should now be at a peak, ready to be directed where it will produce the most rewards and satisfaction. If he were to be clear about cherished goals and aims, plans made now should have a successful outcome. Or so he thought.

On the surface Janice seemed as though she was a self-assured woman. But for some reason she was afraid of some of the folks at her workplace. George in particular was one of them, and whenever he would snap his fingers she would come running, even though he didn't have any direct authority over her. He may have wanted to cultivate a relationship with her himself even though both parties knew it couldn't happen. At some point she came to the conclusion that although never before did she have to make up her mind between a potential relationship with a workmate or her job, she felt this could be the case now. It wasn't really, but to her it had seemed that way. The innuendos involved pointed to George as one of several participants in the gossip fest, which was spooky in its own right. At that point everybody knows that Bruce has a rather intense interest in Janice, and that George, Gloria and a few others would get their kicks by spreading enough gossip to chase him out.

A close, committed relationship with someone was not in the cards for Bruce at this time, as his mindset is not under positive stars. He is too numbed over the conspiracy which was the undoing of his job and his opportunity to get to know Janice better. His goal was to make sure to spend time alone with one whom he hoped could be the love of his life to strengthen ties of affection.

While reading through the local papers at the library, he learned that a social group was sponsoring a picnic this weekend. For a fleeting moment he thought it might be nice to attend, but although feeling lonely inside, he declined. He knew his mindset was not tuned toward meeting new people.

Knowing he may soon have a case to fight, he felt that research work might be beneficial if not enjoyable. He would attempt to dig for information from original sources and if possible, eyewitnesses. Yet at the same time he couldn't help but remember when he felt as if he could go places, and that Janice could assist in the effort.

102

A SIGNIFICANT SIGN OF the time was evident to Bruce, when he went to the unemployment office to use the computers and check to see if any recruiters were going to be there. Not only was there a long line there at the office, but at the same time the computers had been shut down. Folks who asked about this were told that funding had been cut for them. As it was a nice summer day he walked the eight blocks or so from where he lived, and ended up having to turn around and head back. Outside he complained to a woman who was smoking a cigarette about how hard things were. "I know, she responded, "I have sent out lots of resumes without any response."

Many nights these days he would stay up until midnight or later trying to read, listen to music, or just meditate. Even though this summer has for the most part been cooler than usual, he is having a fitful time trying to get to sleep at night.

"That woman's just like me," Bruce thought to himself in regards to the brief conversation he had with her in regards to the employment scene. Apart from possible aggravation this morning, Bruce was hoping for positive trends forthcoming. He had to hope that nobody with whom he were to engage in conversation with were to ask him things such as "Who do you love?" Still wishing that Janice would be his baby, he would try and evade that question as best he could, not yet wanting to wear his heart on his sleeve.

He was to receive some disturbing news once he checked his email. He received a message stating that, regarding his appeal to the corporate office of Cadence Staffing, that the matter was looked into, a proper investigation was conducted, and that the matter was considered closed. This was really a low blow, as he had been quite optimistic after talking to this woman on the phone a couple of weeks back. Now he will have to figure out how to proceed from here.

The people behind the plot must have used a persuasive tongue and manner to be able to convince Cadence not to give in to Bruce. A couple of them, including George, the perceived ringleader, would only have to snap his fingers and they would come running. He was very persuasive and influential even with Matt, the production manager. They were no doubt led to believe that doing so can lead to a few extra perks or treats coming their way. To themselves, however, they felt that nobody they know is as slick talking as he and to some extent his assistant, Gloria. They felt that he could be one who can sell for a living. And if he is as persuasive as he has been with this venture, he could always expect additional sales.

Only the psychic readers he spoke to knew how lonely he felt over this. He has been through stormy periods before, but never one as long-lasting as this one has been—feeling like an island bordered on all sides by nothing.

Bruce now can recall a recent reading he had in which he had been advised that negotiations should proceed successfully for those trying to close a deal or settle a dispute. The latter situation is very much on his mind. Although he could look through any window and see bright sunshine, it might just as well be pouring rain. He is grieving over losing the friendship with Janice, who could get his heart fluttering every time she walked into the room. He is not sure he'll ever be able to sense that again, and despite his feelings of isolation has no real desire to go out to meet new people right now.

Hoping never to be in a position where he would have to make up his mind about things such as this, he would now need to find the star which could guide him on his next move. He was let down because he thought that negotiations should have proceeded successfully for him and that he would be able to close a deal and settle this dispute. But it was not to be, at least not at this particular point in time.

Out of necessity Bruce's focus now moves from pleasure and good times to practical concerns and employment conditions. He would look back at the informal diary he made and saw that back on April 19 he had been approached by another staffing agency about a data entry position, and even went to take the tests and was told that he had passed. But yet the job never came through. He had continued to send out resumes from time to time but never heard anything in return. One day out of the blue he decided to phone Susie, his contact at this agency. She told him that for some reason the company never went through with the job.

Bored by the lack of meaningful activity in his life he would embark on an exercise program. With the beginning of the semi-retirement chapter of his life, he spent more time watching television. In the course of doing so he heard people telling him that he should pay more attention to health, dietary habits, and fitness. So for the next four weeks he would see if this would pay dividends.

103

THE PSYCHIC READER BRUCE started out with was one who would talk too much, therefore running up the bill. Still in need of advice on these issues which have been plaguing him, he would switch readers and would get a response he felt encouraging. The reader told him that someone should come forward shortly and would set the record straight. This made him feel like dancing, but he would not act on this. He did learn of an oldies music show taking place nearby, and did attend it for a time in an attempt to take his mind off the dour facts of his life. He still thought of Janice more than he would want to say, and the reader seemed to indicate to him that they would reconnect someday. While at the outdoor show he asked one lady if she wanted to dance, and to his surprise received an affirmative response. With a positive connection between the two of them, this evening would get off to a good start. They both got plenty of exercise jumping around the dance area.

Hoping she could get his mind off Janice, Bruce would talk with her further after the music stopped. But she relayed to him that there was one she recently split from whom she wishes was back in her arms again. She added that home and domestic affairs may be of some concern as her ailing mother is coming to stay with her, which might provide good excuse to head off to the mall to purchase new furniture, carpeting or curtains to enhance the overall aesthetic appeal of living conditions.

She indicated that she came out to escape some of her own problems, which was the same circumstance as he was in. As he was convinced he was not going to get a phone number, he chose to wrap it up and head for home.

The ride home would find him passing by a young woman who was trying to hitch a ride home. The urge to be of service to other people was strong, and he was tempted to stop if only to warn her of the potential danger involved in doing this.

Upon his arrival home he fell into deep thought. He really hoped that the young woman he saw was safe. He agonized over not stopping for her, if for no other reason than that he would have had the chance to show off his true colors and give something back to one of those in need.

Although he did elect to take Social Security, he would still have money issues with no substantial job prospects coming his way. He thought that a small bet at the track or casino could boost his cash flow. But he felt that would be too risky, so he settled on a lottery ticket.

While reading the local paper he saw an ad for a social club for single folks. The contact person was a lady named Caroline. Bruce would phone her to see if there was still space available, and there was. Thoughts would now turn to the phase of his life when he was a traveling man, first during vacations and then living in different places when he would go looking for such activities.

While he felt that a social occasion could be enjoyable, his spirit was still occupied by so many memories of Janice and the downfall of his job that he felt out of shape. Although he felt he should get out and meet people, in the end an early night may appeal more than staying out partying to the wee hours of tomorrow morning.

104

DID JANICE REALLY HAVE responsibility for Bruce being forced to hit the road, or did the others in her circle make more out of the episode than really existed? This nagging question forced his mind and spirit to wander a lot. It proved to bother him a great deal, but he was just as bothered by the aftermath, not sure of which way to turn. By nature he possessed very limited powers of persuasion, but now he would launch his own crusade to see what kind of help he could get to achieve a resolution. He would begin to pursue this at a steady pace in the hope that if he kept at it bright ideas should be forthcoming. His imagination would be working overtime as his mind moves through the sign of trying to explain the original scenario to those who could help him. For once in his life he would feel a sense of power, which the psychic readers he spoke to said would prevail. After spending money to self-publish two books he didn't really have resources to spend on lawyers and/or private investigators.

But it wouldn't be long before this feeling of power would be replaced by that of a ball and chain. None of the groups he spoke with felt that he had a case because it didn't fall within the guidelines of legally protected situations like race, age, or sexual orientation. But those around him encouraged him to hang on, and that he would receive justice someday. As one currently grappling with a problem, he felt as though he should find that help is available. But for now it has eluded him, and even on sunny days he felt his heart was full of rain. And while the summertime has traditionally been his most active social season, this year has for sure been the exception, and there seemed to be no cure for his bout of the blues. Maybe he was in over-reactive mode, but true justice continued to elude him. By viewing a situation from all angles, he felt that it shouldn't take long to find a satisfactory solution. But such would continue to not occur, pushing him further into despair.

The urge to express himself now would lead Bruce to short bursts of activity. With a sense of belonging usually being elusive, he would express feelings more in writing, although for the most part his muses were not related to actual experience. While he misses the more wild days of the past, with no job prospects and money issues, he has doubts that he will ever be able to return there. Still, variety will be essential to keep his motivation high. But he cannot take risks with finances. So he is forced to retreat by spending much time at home and at the local library where he seeks out particularly social justice sites through which he hopes to find some answers to his issue. Even though Janice no longer has him shaking all over, he still has not lost the desire to be able to set the record straight. But as time goes on he wonders more and more if justice will elude him for good and will he even go to his grave not knowing.

Since Janice has been gone from his life Bruce has been sullen a good share of the time. His efforts to find other work have gone for naught, and at times he has wondered if it was worth trying so much. Minor luck would come his way with the arrival of fall, when he landed a temporary job in a publishing company. He established a good rapport with Susie, the woman who was for the most part in charge of the project. She told him and the other person working along with him that they were the best team she ever had there, and that she wanted them back next time around. But Bruce's interlude of feeling groovy would be short-lived, and it would be several months before any other real opportunities would come his way. As he was registered with several staffing agencies, he was certain that at least one of them would run to him with some good offers. But the continued calling would leave him coming up empty, wondering where he could now turn.

Step by step, Bruce would make attempts as seeing what he could do to regain some semblance of control over his life's circumstances. However today, unlike yesterday, is the time to steer clear of any type of gambling. That included lottery tickets, even though he did win a fairly substantial prize a few months back (although not a big jackpot). And while social activities or entertainment that provides stimulation and excitement should be the first choice for amusement, because of the situation he is in he has to force himself to give such venues a wide berth, especially if substantial expenditure is involved.

105

CONTINUATION OF THE STATUS quo, not knowing for sure what went down, would only serve to make Bruce feel pressured. With him and the agency which employed him in dispute, the upcoming time frame could be full of power struggles and emotional blackmail. Upon one evening near the holiday period, he happened to be wondering what Janice was doing tonight. So he chose to call Carrie Lynn, an advisor on the psychic line he uses in order to find out. While she could sense that this was a concern to him, the conversation went in a somewhat different direction. She could detect and confirm the feelings of emotional blackmail. She did ask him to provide his birthday and also that of Janice if he knew it. She did mention that Janice felt bad that things got out of hand as much as they did. She then told him that she does tend to be a wild thing at times, and that could prove to be a detriment should any relationship have developed, and that he may have been lucky that it didn't.

Fortunately, he is not likely to be uncomfortable with this energy, only tripping up when it comes to finishing one task completely before moving on to the next one. Sensing that he was looking to find some green grass somewhere, Carrie Lynn suggested that he try mediation. The conversation ended with her sensing that Janice made him very happy when he assumed that she was attracted to him as much as he was to her, and that the crash that followed has been very hard for him to handle.

As a rule Bruce is one not generally known to scatter his energy, but today could be an exception to that rule unless he were to make focus a priority and not allow others to make a monkey out of him. His living arrangements might need a few changes, as a loved one could demand some serious tender loving care. But not even Laura, the one woman he is on occasion intimate with, has ever been one to demand such attention from him.

In a call to a psychic reader one evening the conversation drifted off into other areas besides the usual. She told him that a home appliance, machinery, or office equipment could break down at the most inconvenient time. At first he was dumbfounded by this, as he lives in a rented room and really has no true appliances or machinery. He has no computer of his own as his budget doesn't allow for said purchase. But he does have one of these smart typewriters he uses to copy some of his writings. It is now over twenty years old and has served him well. Sure enough, it broke down on him as he was trying to do some writings. He phoned a repair facility he had taken it to in the past, and was told that they no longer repair typewriters. By now word processors and personal computers had made typewriters a relic of the past. He has often expressed disdain over the idea that for items such as this and his music system that you can't seem to get anything repaired locally.

106

WHILE SURFING THE INTERNET at his local library Bruce learned about a social activity taking place in the area. He chose to count himself in on this, as he felt the need to move on from the dogma which has plagued him for now nearly a year.

When he received a letter upon his appeal to the corporate office of Cadence informing him that they had considered his case closed, he could have treated this as a death knell. But he felt there had to be another avenue he could travel down in order to get his story out. All he really wants is the opportunity to tell it like it is, and that his attraction toward Janice was in no way meant to disrupt any of the essential work of the facility. Following the advice of one of his readers, he chose to check out the mediation process. A lady by the name of Lucille had contacted him and informed him that the other party had to also be willing to participate, that it can't be a one-sided affair.

Wanting a second opinion he contacted another potential mediator, Eleanor. But she pretty much told him the same thing that Lucille had. What he really wanted was to be able to pull a surprise punch on the people at Cadence, but now it looked as if he wouldn't be able to. And so he would shoot off an email to headquarters and asked to mediate. He received a reply which stated that someone would contact him tomorrow.

When the call arrived he would speak with a man named Peter O'Neill. He seemed to Bruce to be quite sociable at least, and he knew he would need to make the most of the opportunity prevailing today. But even though Peter had a sociable demeanor he would stick to his guns regarding the action taken. He told Bruce that business and pleasure don't usually mix well and that he would be better served in spending time with loved ones in his sphere who can provide emotional comfort rather than getting strung out on a coworker.

Creative juices were now flowing as Bruce would send an email off to Peter describing some details in what would turn out to be a futile attempt to seek some form of exoneration. How can he be sure, Bruce thought, that there was flagrant wrongdoing on his part if he did not fully understand his side of the story? Although Peter passed himself off as a mediator, it seemed obvious to Bruce that he really was not at all interested in bargaining with him in any way. But he was determined to impart any type of information to the powers that be and felt that they should be pleased with his presentation. Although he felt satisfied that his explanation of events was so fine, the silent treatment would prevail—the implication being that the people he was dealing with on both ends were those one couldn't dare mess with. And yet Bruce may choose to tax resources as much as possible, but energy to withstand his demands and persistence would not be in plentiful supply.

One Tuesday afternoon he would meet with a career counselor at the community college which serves his area. And she informed him that in his state he had the right to have access to his employee file. Upon learning this he would head over to the local office in attempt to secure this. But he got no answer that day as they did not get a response from headquarters. Near closing time when he went in to inform them he was going home, the doors were already locked, an implied message for him to hit the road. He did phone a couple of days later and was informed that his file was at corporate headquarters and not the local office.

Many of the psychic readers he spoke to indicated that Janice could someday come back into his life, giving him hope, indicating that there could be a cause to celebrate. And that there would also at least in dreams of grandeur, a social calendar which may overflow with exciting events and glamorous occasions to attend.

But Bruce would find these dreams not to be forthcoming. While not exactly living on the poor side of town, he was nowhere close to being able to afford even what could pass for an average lifestyle. His closest lady friend, Laura, is not one he would consider marriage to. And she probably wouldn't accept anyway, as she is often still dogged by the results of the abusive marriage she was in. Yet sensing the ongoing depression he was in, she invited him over. A home-cooked meal, she figured, could delight her closest loved one outside of family this evening, and there would be a surprise guest as well. That was her friend Sharon, one that she goes on vacation with at times. It would be an enjoyable enough occasion yet nothing spectacular. Upon returning home he would take to writing some new poetry, all the while wishing he had the fortitude of Superman in order to solve his dilemma.

107

SO MANY MEMORIES FLOOD Bruce's mind as he attempts to make sense of his true story of love and multiple loss. For a time, over a dinner of meatloaf and mashed potatoes at a local diner, he sorts through some notes he made while talking to the various psychic readers. A common thread of betrayal and jealousy ran through the readings he had, although they did run the gamut as to who all was responsible. A couple of readers actually pegged Janice as the kingpin, but most had her as having only a minor part in his actual downfall, with most of the dirty work being done by others. One reader in particular tended to give positive readings one time yet negative another time, which caused him to wonder if she cared as much as she had proclaimed.

For intents he was a male version of Little Red Riding Hood, being approached by the Big Bad Wolf in the form of seven key players. The two frontrunners were George Singletary and Gloria Sampson. They were co-conspirators of top caliber who set out to leave Bruce's career in bits and pieces.

Those two even had the audacity to even have an organized party celebrating Bruce's ouster after it took place. Next on the roster of conspirators was Kathy, the close coworker of Janice's who actually helped her to land the job within the facility. She was very expressive, and determinedly would keep the beat going when Janice became unsure as to whether she should say anything regarding Bruce's attraction for her. Kathy somehow developed quite an undercurrent of dislike for him which she did her best to keep him from detecting. As soon as he came clean about the attraction she was ready to pounce on Janice to make sure she didn't let the matter slide.

Then there was Matt, the facility production manager. Janice really was not among his favorites, because she is known as one that would not kiss butt, as the saying often goes. Story has it that she was about ready for the knock of the pink slip on her door, and she may have felt the need to expose Bruce's supposed indiscretions to save her own job.

But Matt may have been the most prejudiced of the bunch where Bruce was concerned, willing to do all that he could to make sure he never returned to the site, all the while keenly aware that he could attempt to put up a fight even though he was not a regular employee. But if he were to try and sue, he was really going to have to go through Cadence. "How sweet it is," he proclaimed once learning that Bruce's tenure was history. Ariel, an assistant in another office, chose to drop out upon learning of the vicious nature of the plot.

Robin, his work mate at the next station, was the one who most knew of how much he would eat out his heart over Janice. She was a bit of a chameleon, however, camouflaging her true feelings in order to blend in with the prevailing mood. She nearly took it personal when one day he expressed some feelings for Janice to her. Even though Robin had someone in her life she still showed some jealousy over the attention.

Next up was Tim, her pseudo boyfriend on the scene. Even though there was no real relationship with Janice off-campus, he did possess some desire to get next to her on a deeper level. One thing he and Bruce did have in common was that both of their parents had met at work, and in both cases their dad had been their mom's boss at work. And that was also true of Janice and Bruce, even though she was only his lead and not the true department supervisor.

The last of the un-magnificent seven was Samantha, his representative from Cadence Staffing, who was the manager of that particular account. When, upon receiving his employee file from their corporate office, a letter was attached accusing him of making frequent visits to the local office, he was certain that Samantha had something to do with this, as they have had words before, going back to the saga of the bogus email. It was as though a thousand eyes were prying on his movement.

Bruce accepted this job assignment in the spirit that on each morning this was another day when a bright and positive attitude can attract opportunities his way. Extra effort, he reasoned, could help to ensure success with a project that many were struggling to complete. Little did he anticipate that a knife with a jagged edge would lurk behind the scenes, ready to cut his career to pieces. Seven different people took turns using the knife, each cutting in their own way.

Come judgment day, Janice was dressed in what could almost pass as party dress, at least within Bruce's mind. And he is certain that this was all done as a set-up, especially with the main operations being brought down for an hour in such a deadline-charged facility. Through the subsequent time frame he has questioned how he would react toward Janice if he saw her again. And on most occasions his response was that he would launch what attempt he could to get the record set straight on both sides. He knows that he will never feel vindicated until this is done.

He learned one day of a gypsy woman who gives readings at a place not far from him. He went to see her one day but came away feeling less than satisfied, and swore that he would never go again. Frustrated by his inability to get the results he was seeking, he chooses to resume life as best he could. He has self-published two paperbacks he was the writer of; he has made no real money off them. And now his ordeal seems more hindrance than help.

Over time he is forced to shut down life as he knew it. And while he has visions of seeking a lady who could be his, lack of funds coupled with the fallout over how Janice or at least the conspirators socked it to him, his desire to pursue a social agenda would crash. He does connect with one woman through an online dating site whom he meets in the city on a moonlit night. She was a fitness fanatic and that isn't his style although he does do his share of walking during good weather in order to conserve energy.

As time went on and his depression deepened, it became even less likely that Cupid's arrow would ever strike. And the syndrome of hopelessness would lead him to become very withdrawn. It came to seem as if he had exhausted whatever battery of options he may have had. He was reminded of that song about how one fought the law and the law won. He sought out counseling but couldn't afford even the sliding scale fee for his income category although only a fraction of the standard rate.

Bruce Baldwin continues to search in bewilderment, wondering if he will go to his grave never learning the true story.

THE END

JUDAS TIMES SEVEN

Something brewing beneath the surface
Is beginning to haunt me
Her personal attention
Has created jealousy

Trends encouraged spending time alone
So whatever chance Id get
Because I may not have opportunities
For solitary jest

A number of influences prevailing
It would be all-systems-go
And al all-out blast of betrayal
Would force me to spend time at home

Ambitions were on the rise now
That assertive Mars has entered
Everything would be looking up
For my downfall to begin

There were a number of conflicts
With authority figures
But some would welcome this happy day
When my career came to an end

There were three men and four women
Who had set out to betray
Lord I never saw it coming
And I'm baffled to this day

There was no way for me to be prepared
For tension or arguments
They somehow turned the gal against me
Through a silent treatment test

Personal confidential matters
Often do not proceed smooth
And you should be pleased with the results
When at least you're told the truth

One with intuitive ability
Had to tell me what went down
I had to use this expertise wisely
But Jack fell and broke his crown

And there was no Jill tumbling after
Have heard nothing till this day
To behave in a reckless manner
Can send you packing come what may

Now I'm looking past the glasses
To give my confidence a lift
But I'm wishing she'd come clean
And make amends

Attraction can't be regulated
Even if it's not on sale
And I'll wonder till my dying day
The reason for the whole betrayal
And I'll wonder till my dying day
The reason for the whole betrayal